CRASH COURSE!

Frank and Joe paddled furiously, but the current had the raft and wouldn't let go.

Frank threw a quick look back at the sniper. He was gone.

Then Wendy screamed.

Wedged between the rocks lining the ridge of Niagara Junior were sharp, jagged saw blades.

The raft spun sideways in the current. Then there was a sickening ripping sound, and the raft almost exploded as the saw blades tore through its thick, rubbery skin.

Joe felt himself fly out of the boat and over the rapids. As he tried to look behind him, his own paddle, flung like a javelin by the mighty force of the water, struck him hard on the forehead.

The pressure of the crashing water sucked him under.

Books in THE HARDY BOYS CASEFILES™ Series

Available from ARCHWAY Paperbacks

RIVER RATS

FRANKLIN W. DIXON

AN ARCHWAY PAPERBACK
Published by POCKET BOOKS
New York London Toronto Sydney Tokyo Singapore

AN ARCHWAY PAPERBACK *Original*

An Archway Paperback published by
POCKET BOOKS, a division of Simon & Schuster Inc.
1230 Avenue of the Americas, New York, NY 10020

ISBN: 0-671-56123-5

First Archway Paperback printing April 1997

10 9 8 7 6 5 4 3 2 1

Covert art by John Youssi

Printed in the U.S.A.

IL 6+

Chapter

1

"I think Gehenna Canyon's on the other side of this mountain," Frank Hardy said to his younger brother, Joe. "If I could only see this map." Frank squinted in the faint dawn light filtering through the tall pines.

"Pry your eyes open," said Joe, who was driving. Only a few minutes earlier, Frank had been asleep in the back of their van. All night he and Joe had driven, taking turns behind the wheel, to reach Gehenna Canyon in Montana by daybreak.

"Slow down going around this curve," Frank said.

Joe's foot pressed heavily on the gas pedal as he drove down the steep mountain road. "Chill, Frank. We've waited six months to go on this rafting trip, and I don't want to be late."

"Yeah, leadfoot, I hear you," Frank answered. "But don't floor it going around these hairpin turns, okay?"

Joe jerked the steering wheel sharply to the right, then back again to the left, following the treacherous turns in the narrow two-lane road. Frank grabbed the dashboard and pressed on an imaginary brake with his foot.

Steering around a jagged rock, Joe heard the roar of a truck engine behind him. Frank spun around to look out the back window of the van as Joe's eyes darted toward the rearview mirror.

"Look out, Joe!" Frank yelled. "There's a truck on our tail."

A bright blue pickup, its headlights off, careened down the twisting mountain road, gaining on the Hardys' van. Frank saw two men in the truck's cab. The truck was towing a trailer with what appeared to be two small boats covered in canvas.

Joe glanced quickly at the speedometer. "Those guys must be doing seventy," he said.

Frank wasn't listening. His gaze was fixed on the truck as its horn began to blare.

"They're not slowing down!" Frank shouted. "Pull over."

"Where?" Joe asked. "Do you see any shoulder on this road?" The truck's horn blasted longer and louder as the blue pickup gained on the van.

Frank's sharp eyes spotted a small dirt grade

on the opposite side of the narrow mountain road. "Over there!" he said.

Joe jerked the steering wheel to the left and hit the brakes. The van rumbled over rocks and splintered timbers before it thudded to a halt. The blue truck whizzed past them in a cloud of dust, its horn blasting away. The driver turned his head and yelled something at the Hardys. Neither Frank nor Joe could hear what the man said, but they had a good idea of what he meant.

"Stupid idiot!" Joe said, smacking the dashboard with the heel of his hand. "And you thought *I* was a reckless driver."

Frank jumped out of the van and looked at the tires. Among the rocks and broken branches were slivers of green and brown glass. "Guess what, Joe? We've got a flat tire."

One hour later Frank and Joe pulled into a dirt parking lot, beside which stood two log cabins. A small brown wooden sign on the larger cabin said Watson's Big Bison River Rafting Tours. Beneath it hung a smaller metal sign, which read Save the Canyon Foundation.

As Joe turned off the van's engine, he gazed out the window. The log cabins were set against majestic pines that reached up toward the mountains. In front of the cabins ran a wide river that disappeared into a craggy valley. Frank opened the door and breathed a deep sigh as Joe said to no one in particular, "We made it."

Owen Watson, a burly man with a salt-and-pepper beard and a nut brown tan, came out of the larger cabin and ambled toward the Hardys' van. "I was beginning to think you guys got cold feet."

"Not a chance," Frank said as he swung out of the van. He quickly stretched his trim, toned six-foot-one frame and ran his fingers through his short brown hair. Frank walked over and took Watson's outstretched hand. "We almost came into the canyon the short way," Frank said. "Straight down."

Joe jumped out of the van and flexed the tension out of his broad shoulders. He stood an inch shorter than Frank, and his build was more muscular.

"A pair of bozos in a pickup nearly ran us off the road, and we got a flat," Joe said to Owen as they shook hands.

Owen raised an eyebrow. "Blue pickup? Pulling a trailer?"

"Yeah," Frank said. "You know it?"

Owen's jaw tensed. "It belongs to a father-and-son team, Artis and Gordo Haney. Artis is a car dealer in Gehenna. In fact, the *only* car dealer in Gehenna. It's not exactly a metropolis. Gordo works as a mechanic for his dad."

"What kind of boats were on the trailer?" Frank asked Owen.

"They're not boats, exactly. You'll see them once we're on the river," Owen said wearily.

"Unless we're lucky on this trip. Oh, well. I'll bet you guys are hungry."

"We ate breakfast in the van on the way," Joe said with an eager grin. "What we really want to do is hit the rapids."

Owen's face brightened and he said, "That's what I like to hear. First we'll do a short morning ride, just so I can see if you know what you're doing, on some little bitty rapids. We'll have lunch downriver, then come back. You guys can get settled in your cabin this afternoon. Tomorrow we'll hit the really hairy stuff, the white-knuckle rapids." He turned and called into the cabin, "Wendy! Is the gear ready?"

Out of the cabin came a tall, lean girl with a deep tan and shoulder-length brown hair. She looked about seventeen, and the well-toned muscles of her arms showed that she had spent years rowing on the fierce waters of the Big Bison River. She carried a large camera bag over one shoulder and lugged a green-and-white plastic cooler and a canvas duffel bag. "Ready if you guys are," the girl said with a confident air.

Owen turned toward Joe and Frank. "Guys, this is my daughter, Wendy. She's the one who put together the videotape I sent you. Great video, don't you think?"

Wendy rolled her eyes skyward. "Come on, Dad. I'm, like, amateur city."

"Not many rafting operations as small as mine even have a video to send out," Owen said. He beamed at his daughter, then looked back at the brothers. "Wendy, meet Joe and Frank Hardy."

Wendy put the cooler on the ground and shook their hands. "So you're Dad's next victims, huh? Well, if you buy the farm shooting the rapids I'll have it all on tape," Wendy joked, patting her camera bag.

Owen scowled. "Look, Wendy," he said, "I thought we settled this. You're not—" He turned back apologetically to the Hardys. "Would you guys mind putting this cooler and the duffel in the raft? It's down at the riverbank. Make sure to tie the gear down securely. Then you'll find some life vests in my cabin over there. Helmets, too. I'll be right over to give you my famous safety lecture."

Realizing that Owen wanted a moment with Wendy, Frank said, "No problem." He turned to pick up the cooler and noticed that Joe wasn't moving. He was staring at Wendy.

Frank tugged Joe's arm. "Come on, river rat. I thought you wanted to shoot the rapids ASAP."

Joe followed Frank to the riverbank, where they tossed the cooler and the duffel bag into the raft. Turning to look back at Owen and Wendy, Joe said, "I think they're having an argument. I hope Wendy wins. That means she'll be coming along with us."

"Do me a favor, Joe," Frank said. "Remember what we came to Montana for—the river. I don't want to have to explain anything to Vanessa."

Joe grinned at the mention of his girlfriend back in Bayport, Vanessa Bender. "Hey, dating Vanessa doesn't mean I'm married to her, right? Not like you and Callie."

Frank ignored Joe's jibe and started to walk toward Owen's cabin.

Joe strapped the cooler and duffel bag to the inside of the raft, then turned to his brother. "Besides, it would be fun to have a videotape of our trip, wouldn't it?"

Fifteen minutes later, after Owen's thorough safety briefing, Joe and Frank were on the riverbank in their life vests. They pushed the raft into Big Bison River, then jumped into the shallow water. Frank looked back toward the cabins and saw Owen and Wendy coming toward the raft.

"All right!" Joe said softly, so that only Frank could hear.

But Frank couldn't hear Joe at all. A loud drone echoed through the canyon, getting louder by the second.

Frank patted Joe on the shoulder and pointed up the river. Off in the distance two small boats skimmed the surface of the water, making a blaring, raucous sound. As they approached at breakneck speed, Joe figured out what they were. "Cool! Jet-boats!" he shouted to Frank.

Owen broke into a dead run toward the riverbank. "Get out of the water!" he tried to shout over the roaring sound.

7

"What?" Joe yelled.

"Into the raft! Fast!" Owen shouted back. The noise grew louder and louder.

Frank recognized the men riding the boats— Artis and Gordo Haney. Neither of the two was watching where the boats were headed. Their eyes were on Owen Watson.

The boats were almost flying on top of the shallow water. Gordo Haney, the son, rode on the smaller boat—a red-and-white craft about ten feet long that had handlebars like a motorcycle. He sat on a bright red saddle with his feet nestled inside the boat's sleek hull.

The older man's white-hulled boat was a bit larger. Artis Haney sat in the rear on a bright yellow saddle, clutching black handlebars. In front of him were two empty passenger seats. Both boats skimmed the choppy surface of the river, throwing up fan-shaped sprays of white water behind them.

As the jet-boats were almost on top of them, Frank and Joe leaped into the raft on top of the gear.

"Get off my river!" Owen screamed at the two boaters.

Gordo and Artis raced their motors and swerved in the direction of the raft, violently flinging sheets of water over the raft, the gear, and Joe and Frank.

"It's *our* river too, Watson!" Gordo shouted as the boats raced away down the canyon.

Wendy and Owen leaped into the river and helped the Hardys pull the raft back onto the bank. "Those were the bozos who nearly ran you off the road," Owen said. "They've been causing a lot of trouble with my rafting trips. I thought they were heading right for you guys."

"What were those things they were riding?" Frank asked.

Wendy piped up. "Those things are what's ruining the river for us floaters."

"Some people call them personal watercraft or jet-boats, but most people around here call them river jets," Owen said.

"Are they like Jet Skis?" Frank asked.

"Not exactly," Owen replied. "They're small boats with V-eight jet engines—some up to a hundred horsepower. They can do over sixty miles an hour. You can run some of the blasted things in less than a foot of water."

Joe's eyes brightened. "Sounds like fun to me!" he said.

Wendy glared at him. "Wait till we're out on the river," she said grimly. "Then you'll see just how much fun they can be."

Owen flashed a bright smile. "Don't worry about those guys. They won't bother us again. Let's hit the river."

The inflated raft glided silently down the water. Owen Watson, perched in the back of the float, watched carefully for rocks and boulders. Frank and Joe, sitting on either side of the raft with their paddles, gaped at the massive cliffs on both banks of the sparkling Big Bison River. Wendy, nestled next to her father, scanned the horizon with her video camera.

"Take a good look, guys," Owen said to the Hardys. "The Big Bison's one of the most unspoiled places on our planet . . . for now. Enjoy it while it lasts."

Wendy turned her video camera away from the high cliffs and focused on Joe. "Smile, Joe!" she said.

Joe turned to look at Wendy, but Owen barked a command from his vantage point in the back of the raft.

"Boulder to port, Joe. Paddle!"

Joe whipped around and saw a jagged rock coming up fast on the left. He paddled furiously, and the raft pulled off in the opposite direction just in time.

"Always keep your eyes on the river," Owen said firmly. "You can't rubberneck when we go over the rapids tomorrow."

"How do those river jets get on the Big Bison?" Frank asked Owen. "We had to wait six months to get a boating permit from the state forest service."

"Technically, they're not boats because they don't have propellers," Owen said. "It's a legal loophole. I'm regulated, they're not. I get really steamed over it. You heard the racket they make. You smelled the fumes. You saw the wake. What do you think that does to the river?"

Wendy turned to her father. "Dad, chill. Joe and Frank are *floaters,* and they're here for a good time. They don't want to hear your—"

"Frank! Rocks to starboard!" Owen barked. After Frank deftly paddled to avoid the approaching boulders, Owen grinned at the brothers. "You two really know your stuff. I can assure you, we're in for a fun week."

A moment later Owen said, "Okay, we're about to hit our first rapids."

The gentle gurgling of the calm river had turned into a hissing rush. The water churned into white gushes as it crashed over rocks.

"Keep to starboard and hang on!" Owen shouted. The raft started to pick up speed as it careened over the small rapids. Joe and Frank steered the bouncing raft away from the biggest of the rugged rocks. Ahead they saw the stream narrow and move faster as it cascaded between two huge granite boulders.

"Okay, now, jockey us between those two rocks," Owen commanded. "Don't let us hit on either side!"

Frank and Joe tensed themselves for some fast paddling when they heard a throaty rumble in the distance, growing swiftly louder.

"Hang on!" Owen yelled.

Joe looked up to see a river jet zipping upstream between the two boulders at full throttle. The river ran faster and faster through the boulders, propelling the raft into a narrow space that left no room for error. Joe paddled like crazy as the river jet barreled straight toward the raft.

Chapter

2

ARTIS HANEY'S RIVER JET rammed straight into the raft with a roar and a thud. The raft spun around and hit the right side of the pass. As it smacked against the huge boulder, Wendy tumbled out into the icy water. Her video camera went flying too.

Owen reached over the edge of the raft and caught his daughter's hand, but Wendy resisted him. "My camera!" Wendy shouted as she broke loose from his grip. The river jet whizzed past, spraying water everywhere.

Frank and Joe had swung the raft sideways against the boulders, and the swiftly rushing current of the river held it shakily against the rocks. Frank saw Wendy's video camera bouncing violently against the boulder before it began to sink.

"Got the camera!" Frank shouted to Wendy, as he snagged the handle of the video camera with his paddle and maneuvered it into the raft. "I hope it's waterproof," he said.

Owen had pulled Wendy back into the raft. "Push us back into the current and ease us between the boulders," Owen called to Joe and Frank. "We'll try to get to shore."

The Hardy brothers shoved the raft away from the rocks and let the swift current pull it forward. Frank stuck his paddle down into the water and pivoted the raft until it pointed through the pass again, while Joe paddled to dodge the boulders on the raft's left side.

"Not so hard!" Owen shouted at Joe. Joe had paddled so strongly that the front end of the raft was now lodged against the right boulder. "Frank, just push very gently away and we'll—"

Then, out of nowhere, Gordo's river jet thundered between the rocks and hit the front of the raft. This time there was a sickening *r-r-rip* as the aluminum frame of the river jet caught the raft's rubberized canvas.

As the violent wake of the jet-boat crashed against the raft, it flipped over, dumping Owen, Wendy, Frank, and Joe into the river.

Gordo made a swift loop back and circled close to the upended raft. His wake washed over the four floaters, who scrambled to hold on to the raft. Joe thought he spotted the young man thrusting a hunting knife into his pocket. This was no accident, Joe thought. He heard Gordo laugh as the river jet's drone faded into the distance.

The raft was upended between the two boulders, spanning the gap between them, forming an instant dam in the river. Its front half was deflating, flapping against the boulders as the river rushed past.

Frank, Joe, and Owen clung firmly to the raft. "Hey, where's Wendy?" Frank asked.

"Over here, guys!" came the answer. Wendy was about ten yards downriver, swimming in the shallows toward the bank, clutching her video camera to her chest.

"You guys all right?" Owen asked.

"Just a little wet, that's all." Frank said. He and Joe had made their way into the waist-deep water, both holding on to the rapidly deflating raft.

"Okay, campers," Owen shouted glumly. "Let's haul this mess over to shore."

As Owen and Frank finished patching the tear in the front of the raft, Wendy and Joe wrung the water out of the canvas duffel bag. They had spread the gear that was inside it out on the ground. Joe picked up a hand air pump. "Good thing you brought this," he said to Owen.

Owen grunted. "I'm prepared for almost anything."

"I'm afraid to look at the videotape," Wendy

said as she picked up her dripping camera bag. Brushing wet hair from her face, she said, "But the camera *is* waterproof. And this isn't the first time it's been soaked. I just hope I got at least some of that attack on tape and that the tape survived."

The rafting party were sprawled on the river-bank in a cove sheltered by the surrounding cliffs. From their location, they couldn't see too far up or down the river. It was almost noon, and the bright summer sun beat down like a blunt force.

Joe opened the cooler and poured its contents onto the bank. "Too bad the lid came open. I really needed one of those sandwiches." Four soggy sandwiches and a gooey pile of what had been potato chips flopped onto the ground, fol-lowed by a small carp, which flipped and wiggled its way through the grass on the riverbank and then plunged back into Big Bison River.

"You shouldn't have let that fish get away," Frank said to his brother. "That was our best shot at lunch."

"Gordo, you idiot!" Wendy shouted up the river. Her angry voice echoed through the canyon.

Owen came over to his daughter's side. "That's one of the reasons I didn't want you to come along today."

"I know, but it's not like I'm never going to run into him," Wendy said. She turned to Joe and Frank. "I used to date Gordo—the creepy son," she explained.

"Is that why they have it in for you?" Frank asked Owen.

"No," Owen answered. "It has more to do with our Save the Canyon work. I should have prepared you two for something like what just happened. Those Haneys and some of the other river jet-boaters have declared open season on us floaters."

"Why?" Joe asked.

"Well, I want this area to be declared a national park. But if that happens, the government will ban those river jets from the Big Bison completely. You can understand why that makes some people angry. But I'm angry, too. I mean, you two drove all the way out here from—where is it again?"

"Bayport," Joe said. Wendy held the video camera so that she could watch the playback.

"Really?" Wendy smiled at Joe. "I went to Bayport once. My mom's cousin used to live there. Nice place."

Frank noticed that Owen scowled slightly when Wendy mentioned her mother.

Owen continued. "You expected some kind of back-to-nature adventure on the river, right?"

"Something like that," Frank said.

"The canyon hasn't changed in thousands of years," Owen said. "There are still lots of wild animals—mountain lions, bears, moose. Sometimes I get out on the river and can't believe I'm living in this century, till guys like those blasted Haneys come along."

Owen sat quietly for a moment, scanning his gaze across the majestic, wooded bluffs on either side of the clear, sparkling river. Then he spoke again.

"See, the state forest service only allows me to take one group of river rats a day on the Big Bison, but those river jets can come and go any time, anywhere. No speed limits, no restrictions. They're ruining the whole experience, not to mention my business. Don't get me wrong, I'm doing okay, but I'd really like to expand. Hire more guides, take out more rafts . . ."

"I got 'em!" Wendy shrieked with joy as she peered through the viewfinder. "Take a look, Dad."

Owen looked into the camera. "Great, Wendy! That's just what we need."

"Need for what?" Frank asked.

"The whole point of the videos is to get enough hard evidence of the river jets bothering us floaters," Wendy chimed in. "Then we can make a real case that they're a menace. It's an uphill battle."

"Those river jets are only one of the problems on the river," Owen continued. "There are acres of old-growth forest on both banks that the loggers in the area would kill to get their chain saws on. Not to mention what the developers and strip miners want."

Owen was cut off by the sound of more river jets. This time a pack of four of the water vehicles streamed by. Owen stood still while they passed, waiting for the irritating sound of their unmuffled engines to fade into the distance.

"Did you recognize anybody in that bunch?" Owen asked his daughter.

"No," Wendy said. "At least it's not the Haneys."

Joe stood holding Wendy's camera. "Shouldn't you have been taping them?" he asked.

"Only if there's some kind of disturbance," Wendy replied. "As long as we're not in the water, there's nobody for them to disturb. They'd all be happier if we went away."

"I still think it looks like it could be fun," Joe said, knowing that Owen and Wendy were about to jump down his throat. "Just, um, not on Big Bison River," he added. "I mean, in the right time and place."

Wendy smiled. "I agree with you, Joe, and so do most of the people around here. Dad's the extremist in the bunch. He thinks they should be outlawed everywhere."

"Don't go pushing my buttons," Owen said to Wendy, "unless you want to hear me go into overdrive about the environment again."

"Can it, Dad. We're all too wet and hungry," Wendy said. As she began to pack her video equipment, she asked, "How soon will that patch be set so we can get back on the river?"

Owen walked over to the raft and tapped his finger on the thick gray patch over the rip in the front pontoon. "I think it's set. Bring me the pump, and we can be back on the river in a couple of minutes."

Frank picked up the air pump from the ground and handed it to Owen. "Watch the patch, Frank, and make sure it holds," Owen said. The river guide started to pump air into the pontoon but abruptly stopped. Frank saw the burly man turn his head upriver and freeze.

The four floaters heard the roar of a river jet engine once again coming from upriver.

"Get the camera going," Owen called out to Wendy. She quickly pulled out her camera, rolled the tape ahead, and started shooting. Gordo Haney was coming back downriver on his river jet at top speed. He whizzed past the bank where the Watsons and the Hardys were standing. He didn't even turn his head to look at them.

Owen ran into the shallow water near the riverbank and shouted at Gordo, "Get off my river! I've had it with you guys! You wreck one more of my tours and I'll—"

Suddenly a shot rang out. Frank saw Owen clutch his side and gasp. Racing into the river's edge, Frank reached for the man just as Owen collapsed into the water.

Chapter

3

FRANK DRAGGED OWEN OUT of the water. As he did, he scanned the cliffs around them. Wendy and Joe ran up to them as Owen moaned in pain.

The unseen sniper fired another shot.

"Hit the ground!" Frank shouted. They all dropped to the rough stones on the bank. Frank did his best to shield Owen's body.

One more shot rang out. Frank tried to locate where it came from, but the resounding echo in the canyon made it impossible to trace.

Somewhere in the distance a boat engine started up, then roared away. A tense few seconds passed silently, with everyone frozen in place.

"Dad! Are you all right?" Wendy said breathlessly.

"Get me back to camp," Owen Watson groaned through his clenched teeth.

As Frank and Joe dragged the raft onto the grassy bank in front of Owen's cabins, the older man groaned in pain. "How are you doing?" Joe asked him.

Lying on his side in the raft, Owen managed a wincing smile. "I've been better." He clutched his hand over the wound on his right side. Frank and Joe had tried to stop the bleeding with their T-shirts, binding them to the wound by tightening Owen's life jacket around his waist.

Frank tied the raft's mooring rope to a post. "Try to hold still, Owen," he said.

Wendy came running out of the cabin. "An ambulance is on its way, Dad," Wendy said. Wading into the shallow water, she grabbed her father's meaty hand and held it tight. "Just breathe slowly," she said.

Owen's face tightened in pain. He looked at Wendy and said, "Promise me you'll go to the town meeting." Wendy told him she would.

An ambulance, its siren wailing, drove into the camp. With swift precision, the paramedics had Owen on a gurney and into the back of the emergency vehicle in a matter of seconds.

"I'm going with Dad to the hospital," Wendy said to Frank and Joe. "Could you guys—"

Frank jumped in. "Don't worry about a thing, Wendy. We'll stow all the gear. Then we'll come find you at the hospital." Frank had already noted the name of the hospital painted on the side panel of the ambulance.

Wendy handed Frank a ring of keys. "Make sure everything is locked up. *Everything.*"

"Sure. The raft, too?"

Wendy's eyes narrowed. "All of it, including the videotape. Just in case somebody comes looking for it." She pointed to a pair of shiny new keys on the ring. "Those are the keys to your cabin. Put your stuff in there."

Joe nodded. "Maybe we should lock the videotape in our cabin."

"Good idea," Wendy said, then turned and climbed into the back of the ambulance.

As the paramedics closed the door and drove away, Joe turned to Frank and sighed. "So much for a peaceful, back-to-nature rafting trip."

Frank scanned the area in a quick circle. "I couldn't tell where that shot came from, but whoever fired it could still be around. Let's get the stuff inside pronto."

"We know it wasn't Gordo Haney. He was on the river when Owen was shot," Joe said. "We all saw him go by."

"Maybe he was a decoy to draw Owen down to the riverbank," Frank said. "We have no idea what's really going on with those Haneys."

Together the Hardys pulled all of the equipment up the low slope to Owen's cabin and took it inside. Then they went back down for the raft, which they carried through the front door. Inside Owen's cabin, Frank and Joe looked around. Rafting equipment all but filled the large front room. A large metal rack held four deflated rafts. Joe and Frank deflated their raft, then heaved it onto the top rack.

An open metal cabinet held a half dozen life jackets. Here and there were coolers, oars, pumps, hip waders, a couple of inner tubes, and some fishing tackle. On the walls were large maps of Big Bison River and the Gehenna Canyon. Along the back wall were three metal file cabinets. In the center of the wall was a heavy wood door.

Joe went over and tugged on the file drawers. "Locked," he said. "I suppose we have the keys on this ring. What do you think's behind the door?"

"Probably Owen's office," Frank said. "But let's not find out now, okay? I think we've already had enough trouble for our first day here. Besides, I'd like to get out of these wet clothes. Then we should get to the hospital and see how Owen's doing. Let's go."

From a distance, the Gehenna Memorial Hospital looked more like a small clinic—two stories tall, drab and functional. When Frank and Joe pulled their van into the parking lot of the hospital, they were hardly prepared for the crowd around the main entrance.

There were only a few cars in the parking lot. Yet bunched around the front door were television camera crews, sound engineers, banks of lights, and a handful of reporters, some with audiocassette recorders. A TV remote link-up van was parked right in front of the building.

A stocky, bald, red-faced man was trying to get the attention of the news crews. He shouted over the confusion, attempting to quiet the crowd. "The hospital will have an official statement for you in about an hour. Till then, we need you all to clear away from the door and move that truck." A general groan came from the crowd.

One reporter pushed in front of the red-faced man. "What about Watson? Is he alive?" the reporter asked.

"As I said, we'll have a statement in one hour," the hospital spokesman said. Then he turned on his heel and went back inside the hospital. The reporters and camera crews started to shuffle away from the door as Frank and Joe made their way against the crowd.

A tall security guard in a blue uniform blocked their way. "No press in the building. Stay outside," the guard said.

Frank didn't move. "We're not reporters. We were with Owen Watson when he was shot," he said. "His daughter is expecting us."

One of the reporters heard what Frank said and turned to the dispersing crowd. "These are

25

the guys who were with Watson!" the reporter bellowed.

Suddenly Frank and Joe were in the middle of a swarm of reporters, all barking questions at the brothers.

"What happened?"

"Did you see who shot him?"

"What did Watson do to make someone want to kill him?"

Bright lights switched on. Cameras began to whir. Joe started to open his mouth when Frank said, "No comment," and pulled Joe toward the door.

"You took the words right out of my mouth," Joe quipped as he and Frank entered the small lobby and faced the security guard again.

"If we're going to find out who did this," Frank said to Joe, "we can't afford to have our faces all over the local news."

The security guard stopped the Hardys again. "Just let me call the intensive care unit and make sure Ms. Watson knows who you are, okay? I've heard all kinds of stories today."

Frank thought that the guard wasn't prepared for the sort of day he was faced with. He also thought to himself that for such a small town, the shooting had created an awful lot of commotion.

Five minutes later the guard came back and led the Hardys to the waiting room, where Wendy sat.

"The nurse from the operating room told me

Dad's out of surgery," Wendy said as Joe and Frank sat beside her. "He's still in intensive care. They may let me see him when he wakes up. But only for a minute or two. Then I'll have to come back tomorrow."

"Are you going back to your dad's camp tonight?" Joe asked.

"I don't know," Wendy said. "I was just staying with Dad to go on your rafting trip. Most of the time I live in town with my mom."

"Got the picture," Frank said.

"I promised Dad that I'd take his place at tonight's town meeting at eight o'clock," Wendy said. "Why don't we look at that videotape before the meeting? Dad's got a VCR in his office. Maybe somewhere in that last shot we'll see the sniper."

"Great idea," Joe said.

A doctor in green surgical scrubs entered the waiting room and walked up to Wendy. "Ms. Watson?" the short, dark-haired doctor asked.

Wendy stood up. "How is he?" she asked quietly.

"We won't know until tomorrow. I couldn't remove the bullet. It's too risky at the present time. All I could do for now was patch him up. When his vital signs are stable, we'll have to go back in."

Wendy bit her lower lip. The doctor's gaze softened. He said gently, "You can speak to him for just a minute when he comes around."

Wendy looked back at Joe and Frank. "Can my friends come in with me?" she asked. When the doctor pursed his lips and looked at the floor, Wendy added, "They were with us when Dad was shot. They helped get him back to shore. I know he'd like to thank them."

The doctor took a deep breath. "Well, okay, but keep it really short. He's been through a lot and needs to rest."

The three rode the elevator to Owen's room. Owen looked pale and groggy as Wendy sat in the flimsy plastic chair at his bedside. The man's eyes shifted toward Frank and Joe, who stood behind Wendy. "Hi, guys," Owen rasped in a faint whisper. "That river was pretty wild today, huh?"

"Don't talk, Dad," Wendy said.

"Owen," Frank said, "we'll do whatever we can to find out who shot you."

"That's right," Joe said. "We've had a lot of experience—"

Owen's eyes narrowed into puffy slits, and he sucked in air and winced. "Don't . . ." he muttered. "You don't know what's going on." The words seemed to take all of his strength.

Wendy leaned forward in her chair. "Calm down, Dad. The doctor said you need to rest." She turned to Joe and Frank. "Would you guys leave me alone with Dad now, please? I'll meet you later at the camp."

Frank and Joe said their goodbyes and offered their help before they left Owen's room.

"Where do we start? Artis Haney and his son?" Joe asked Frank when they reached the door of the intensive care unit.

Frank thought for a moment. "First, let's shake those reporters. Maybe there's a back way out of here."

Frank had turned the corner and started down the stark green corridor when his path was blocked by a tall, broad-shouldered figure in a tan and navy blue uniform.

"You boys aren't going anywhere," the man snarled.

Chapter

4

THE MAN WORE a trooper's hat, but what caught Frank's attention was the officer's flowing, shoulder-length black hair and the ornate silver and turquoise band around his wrist.

Joe couldn't help noticing the man's keen, piercing gaze and his shiny silver police badge.

"If I'm not mistaken," the officer said, "you're mixed up in Owen's shooting. Am I right?"

"Sort of," Joe said. The policeman stared at Joe, waiting for him to say more. "I'm Joe Hardy, and this is my brother, Frank."

The officer sized both of them up. "Chief Billy Two Trees," he offered grudgingly.

"Chief?" Frank asked.

"*Police* chief," the officer said. "Not a chief in my tribe, only in the Gehenna Police Department."

"What tribe is that?" Frank asked.

"Blackfoot. I grew up on a reservation not far from here." The police chief switched right back to business. "I have a few questions for you. I expect some answers, and they'd better be good ones. Follow me."

Chief Two Trees walked past the waiting room where Frank and Joe had met Wendy and continued down a long hall. Joe thought to himself, He must be taking us to a private room to question us. Instead, the chief turned at the hospital cafeteria.

"Have a seat," Chief Two Trees ordered. Frank and Joe sat. "Want a sandwich?" he asked. "Stick to the tuna fish. The roast beef's stringy. The mystery meat burgers are vile."

"Two tunas, I guess," Frank said.

Frank and Joe waited while the police chief came back with a tray of sandwiches and sodas, refusing to take money from the brothers.

"Now tell me everything you know," Chief Two Trees said, leaning back in his chair and folding his arms over his well-muscled chest. "And don't talk with your mouths full."

Joe and Frank recounted, in as much detail as they could remember, all of the day's events. They both tried to be as calm and accurate as possible, for neither Hardy could tell what the police chief's take on the whole matter was.

Frank noticed that the chief didn't take a single

31

note, but silently absorbed every detail and asked the brothers for more information.

"I've already talked to Artis and Gordo Haney," Chief Two Trees said. "Artis has an alibi. He says he was on the riverbank making a call on his cellular phone at the time of the shooting. You say you saw Gordo whiz by on his river jet. What about those other four boaters? You get a good look at them?"

"Not really," Joe said.

Chief Two Trees leaned forward. "Did Wendy get them on tape?"

Joe and Frank looked at each other, both wondering how the man knew about the video camera.

Chief Two Trees continued. "These days three men in a tub can't ride Big Bison River without that girl taping 'em."

"What about Gordo slicing up the raft?" Joe asked. He had explained earlier about seeing the Haney boy with a hunting knife.

Chief Two Trees looked directly into Joe's eyes. "Unless you can prove otherwise, Gordo Haney says the whole thing was an accident. Says *your* party was in *his* way."

Joe turned the van out of the hospital parking lot and onto the main street of Gehenna.

"Owen said that Artis Haney has the only car dealership in town," Frank said. "It shouldn't be too hard to find, since there are only two streets here with any kind of business on them."

In a matter of seconds the van pulled into the main intersection at the town square. Frank looked to the right, Joe to the left. "I see it!" Joe said, making a left turn.

Artis Haney stepped out of his dealership office building to meet Joe and Frank even before the van had stopped moving. He looked about fifty and wore a straw cowboy hat and a white shirt that couldn't conceal a great expanse of belly over his belt. Artis's skin was tanned and leathery. Frank and Joe recognized him instantly, and Artis recognized them.

"You're Watson's pals, right?" Artis scowled.

Frank remained calm and unruffled. "Mr. Haney, we need to buy a new spare tire. We got a flat this morning."

"*Someone* ran us off the road," Joe added.

Haney didn't respond, even though he knew what Joe was referring to. Joe quickly glanced around and spotted Haney's new blue pickup parked near the sales office.

"I don't sell tires," Artis said, squinting as if to keep the bright afternoon sun out of his eyes. "There's a dealer over in the next town, about thirty miles."

Spotting a rack of tires in the dealer's showroom, Frank asked, "What are those?" He pointed toward the tires.

"Just for locals, partner. And what's going on down the river is just for locals, too. I'd advise both of you to let it alone, you get me?"

33

Joe had been keeping quiet too long. "I don't think we can 'let it alone,' Mr. Haney. Owen Watson was nearly killed this morning."

"And it could have been my son," Artis said. "Or me, if my boat engine hadn't conked out upriver."

Gordo Haney came out of the garage just then. He was wearing a grease-stained coverall and a baseball cap turned backward. Frank noticed he carried a long steel pry bar in his hand. Frank thought he and Gordo were about the same age, eighteen.

"These guys causing trouble, Dad?" Gordo asked.

"No trouble, son," Artis drawled. "As long as they move on and mind their own business. And let us tend to ours."

"We came here to ride the rapids," Joe said deliberately. "It's not easy to do if someone keeps slashing our rafts."

Gordo slapped his open palm twice with the pry bar. "I don't know what you're talking about. We had a little collision this morning, that's all. Just an accident."

"That was no accident," Joe said. Frank could sense his younger brother's temper rising.

"Where'd you say that tire dealer was, Mr. Haney?" Frank asked coolly.

"Route eighty-three, right out Main Street. Bear right and follow the signs to Cougar Bend.

They'll close before too long," Artis said. "Better hit the road."

By the time Frank and Joe found the other dealership in Cougar Bend, it was locked up tight. Artis knew that when he sent us here, Frank thought with frustration. They turned the van around and headed back to Gehenna.

During a quick dinner at downtown Gehenna's one and only diner, Frank and Joe rehashed the day's events. When it came time for the check, Joe looked for the waitress, a woman named Claire in a pink uniform. She was a plump, chatty, middle-aged woman who called everyone "Hon." She seemed to know everyone in town, and everyone knew her by name.

Joe walked over to the counter and found Claire hanging up the pay telephone by the kitchen, with her eye on a portable black-and-white television. He handed her the bill and money.

As she gave him his change, Claire mentioned that she had seen Frank and Joe's faces on the news. As Frank joined his brother, Claire asked about Owen. Joe and Frank answered her tersely and turned to leave.

On a bulletin board by the door of the diner, Joe spotted a bright orange sheet of paper advertising jet-boats for sale. All but one of the telephone numbers at the bottom had been torn off.

Joe took the last one, looked at it, then went back into the diner and made a telephone call.

"Okay, Frank," Joe said as he met his brother at the van. "I've got directions to a river jet dealer's. His name's Lee Roy Samuels. His dealership's just outside of town."

"Let's move out," Frank said. "Maybe this guy can tell us about the other jet-boaters we saw on the river today."

Frank and Joe entered the office of Lee Roy Samuels's boatyard a little after six o'clock. Behind the desk sat a man in a red sport shirt watching a small color TV. His hair was cropped in a crew cut.

"Mr. Samuels?" Frank asked. Samuels did not move. "Mr. Samuels, we called about renting a, um, personal watercraft for the week." Samuels held up his hand, palm out, as if to stall Frank and Joe.

"Just a minute," Samuels barked, his gaze fixed on the television screen.

Frank looked at the screen, curious to see what had the man's attention. He was surprised to see a picture of himself and Joe going into Gehenna Memorial Hospital, followed by a shot of the hospital spokesman saying, "Mr. Watson is in stable condition. The local police are investigating the shooting."

As the camera cut back to a reporter, Lee Roy Samuels turned to Frank and Joe. "Well, well,

well," Samuels crowed. "It's the boys from back east that was just on the news. What do a couple of Watson's floaters want with one of my boats?"

"We just want some information, Mr. Samuels," Frank said.

"You want information, pick up the phone and dial the operator," Samuels sneered. "I'm closing up."

"But you might be able to help us," Joe said.

"Help Owen Watson, you mean." Samuels glared at Joe. "I want nothing to do with that river rat. That man is a direct threat to my livelihood!"

"Is that why you shot him?" Joe blurted.

"Now, wait just a minute," Samuels said, rising to his feet. "Did I say anything about shooting the man?"

Frank smacked his brother lightly with the back of his hand and said, "Please, my brother didn't mean—"

"What goes on between me and Watson is strictly business. Your friend Owen Watson makes a nice living off that river, so he should just keep his trap shut," Samuels said. "I don't like the creep, but I'm sorry he took a bullet. Now, if you two will clear out, I got to get home."

"Nice move, boy genius," Frank muttered as the brothers drove toward the center of town.

"I couldn't help myself," Joe said.

Frank drove on in silence for a mile or two. He knew his younger brother was brash and impulsive. Sometimes he even admired him for it. This wasn't one of those times. "Well, we've both had a pretty rough day," Frank said to his brother, clearing the air.

Before long they arrived back at Owen Watson's camp. When Frank pulled out the keys to open their cabin, he saw that the door was already open. He called to Joe, "Go check Owen's cabin."

Joe jumped out of the van and dashed toward the cabin, where earlier he and Frank had locked up the raft and the gear.

Frank pushed open the door to the other cabin. He found the door open and the lights on.

Both of the brothers' suitcases had been pried open, and their clothes were flung all over the floor.

Quickly Frank stuck his hand under the mattress of the top bunk bed.

Wendy's videotape was gone.

Frank ran to Owen's cabin. Through the front window he saw Joe standing still, with his hands in the air.

Frank stopped in the doorway and froze.

Standing in the middle of Owen's cabin was a man wearing a full green camouflage suit and a knit ski mask. The man was pointing a carbine rifle at Joe.

Before Frank could think, the masked man turned and swung his rifle right at Frank's heart.

Chapter
5

"FRANK! DROP!" JOE YELLED as the masked sniper aimed his rifle at Frank.

Frank dropped to the ground just outside the doorway.

The masked man shoved a rolling office chair at Joe. He caught the chair and ducked behind it, using the back of the chair as a shield.

The man then turned and bolted into Owen's office, which was already open. He violently kicked open the back door and ran into the woods behind Owen's cabin.

Frank and Joe both scrambled to their feet and ran to the back door. Somewhere off in the shady woods they heard the sound of a truck engine starting. A pair of red taillights disappeared into the twilight gloom as the truck's driver floored the accelerator.

"Let's call Billy Two Trees," Joe said to Frank.

"So what do you think happened?" Joe asked the police chief after he had surveyed the damage to the cabins.

"Burglary," Chief Two Trees replied tersely.

Another man in a khaki shirt and matching trousers knelt at the lock of the Hardys' cabin. "I can't tell if this lock was picked," said State Forest Service Ranger Roger MacKendrick.

"That's why you're the forest ranger and I'm the cop," Chief Two Trees said dryly. "Don't muck around with the evidence, Roger."

Ranger MacKendrick was a pale, sandy-haired man with intense blue eyes that were his most distinctive feature. Frank guessed from his pasty complexion that MacKendrick spent more time at his desk than outdoors.

"Maybe we'd better get Owen's okay to change the locks," Joe said.

Chief Two Trees carefully dusted the lock and door latch for fingerprints, then said, "Okay, I'm done. You can put your things away," he said to Frank and Joe. "There are no prints on anything. Whoever did this sure didn't want me to find him."

As Frank and Joe started stuffing their clothes into dresser drawers, Wendy walked into the cabin. She had been checking out the damage in her father's place.

"I don't get it. Everything's torn apart. Whoever it was went through all of my video equipment but took only some blank tapes," Wendy said.

Frank then told her that the tape he'd put in his room for safekeeping was gone.

Chief Two Trees stuck his thumbs in his belt and rocked back and forth on the heels of his hand-tooled western boots. "What was on that tape?"

Wendy darted a quick glance at Joe and Frank. "I'm not quite sure. We were going to watch it this afternoon."

Chief Two Trees frowned. "We?"

"We thought we might be able to see who shot Owen by watching the tape," Joe said.

"I can't believe someone would do this to my father," Wendy said, staring blankly into space.

Ranger MacKendrick stood up and nodded gently toward Wendy. "Sorry to bring this up, young lady. But a lot of people are mad at your father over this 'Save the Canyon' business, especially those Knights of Liberty yahoos."

Wendy snapped back to the present. "I know my dad's not Mr. Popularity, but all he wants is to keep the canyon in its pristine state—as a national park."

Joe was puzzled. "Isn't the land protected now?"

"No," MacKendrick said. "We manage the land, but that doesn't mean we guard it. Right now we allow some grazing, some timber cutting, and a bit of development, as long as the basic ecology isn't damaged. Owen doesn't like that, but it's the law."

"What Roger's not telling you is that the state's lease on the land is about up," Chief Two Trees added. "Before it can be renewed, everybody else in town gets to stick an oar in the water—pardon the figure of speech—at tonight's town meeting."

"You mean the locals are *all* against Mr. Watson?" Joe asked.

Chief Two Trees took a deep breath. "I wish it were that simple. Everybody wants something different out of the canyon, and they're all at one another's throats. A lot of them are willing to go to the wall for what they want . . . even if it means taking out Owen Watson and anyone else who stands in their way."

"You mentioned the Knights of Liberty," Frank said. "Who are they? And could they have wanted Mr. Watson out of the way?"

"The Knights are a local militia movement. They want the federal government to keep its nose out of our canyon," MacKendrick answered.

Chief Two Trees laughed heartily. "As my old Blackfoot grandmother says, 'One man puts a penny in a pot, ten others want to take out dollars.' "

Ranger MacKendrick squinted at the chief. "Billy, what in blazes does that mean?"

Chief Two Trees shrugged. "Beats me. Some-

times I think my grandmother's a little loopy."
He turned to Joe and Frank. "If you two want
to see how steamed up the locals get over this
issue, come to the town meeting tonight at
eight o'clock."

After the ranger and the police chief left,
Wendy said she wanted to go home to her mother's. "I feel a little creepy hanging around here,"
she said. "Don't you guys?"

"I can't say we feel too secure out here after
what's happened," Joe said. "But the worst thing
we could do is turn tail and run. That's exactly
what that masked guy wants us to do."

"Okay, then. I'll see you at the town meeting,"
Wendy said.

Later that evening Frank and Joe crossed the
town square and slipped into Gehenna Town
Hall. The main assembly room looked like a
cross between a courthouse and a church base-
ment. The hall was crammed with people. Joe
thought the whole town and half the neighboring
area had been stuffed into the room.

The cool early evening air barely entered the
room, even though the two ancient electric fans
creaked away in a vain attempt to keep a breeze
going. Frank and Joe slipped into a pair of folding chairs tucked into a back corner. At first they
thought that nobody noticed them. Then Frank
caught Chief Two Trees standing in the opposite
corner. He nodded at Frank and Joe.

At the front of the room on a raised platform, a sweaty man in a seersucker suit stood before a microphone. On both sides of him sat half a dozen men in summer suits.

"I know you're all waiting to hear what our first speaker has to say, so let me give the mike over to Mr. Carl Vissen." The man at the microphone stepped away. A taller, silver-haired man rose to his feet and was greeted by a round of applause and a chorus of booing and jeering.

Carl Vissen adjusted the microphone a little higher and began to speak. "Thank you, Mayor Latimer." Vissen waited for the booing to stop. It didn't. Vissen continued. "As you all know, there's been a lot of wrangling lately over the future of the canyon. And there have been a lot of rumors about what my plans are."

Joe felt a light tap on his shoulder. He spun his head around to find Wendy standing right behind him, leaning against the back wall. She stood with a woman who looked just like her, only about twenty years older. Joe figured it must be Wendy's mom. Frank turned and nodded to Wendy, then focused back on Vissen.

Vissen knew how to work a crowd, Frank observed. His delivery was smooth, his manner confident, almost brash. Vissen had the air of a man used to getting whatever he wanted.

"This is neither the time nor the place for me to present my plans in full," Vissen continued. "I'm working with our esteemed Mayor Latimer to schedule another open meeting for that purpose. Tonight I just want to clear up a few things. Some of you have heard that I want to buy up all the land. That's a lie. I want the canyon to remain under state forest service control. But you all know how I like to build things."

A small chuckle rumbled through the crowd along with a few hisses.

"Parts of the canyon should stay available for everyone's use. Some of the more extremist and elitist groups in this area . . ."

Vissen's words were met with more hisses and some scattered applause. But the man continued, unfazed: "Some want to control who uses the river and when they get to use it. My plan will keep the river open for everyone who wants to use it—as long as they play by the rules. But there's a lot of land on both sides of that river . . . land that nobody seems to be using."

"What about us ranchers?" a man in the crowd shouted. "We're using that land right now, Carl!"

Vissen nodded at the man and continued. "We're talking about *profitable* use, Nick. I know your ranchers are grazing their sheep and cattle up on the bluffs, but that's no way to make money."

"That's right, Carl," came a voice from the crowd.

Vissen went on. "Let's face it, folks. Right now the only tourist dollars we're seeing are the few spoiled river rats who come to bounce their brains out going down the rapids. And you all know how little money that brings in."

Frank hunched down in his seat, trying to be invisible. Joe took a deep breath.

"Think what a new Carl Vissen Luxury Resort up on those bluffs would do for the Gehenna Canyon area!" Vissen exclaimed. "More jobs, more tourists, a bright future for the whole region!"

"Can it, Vissen!" an angry voice barked. It was Artis Haney. "Bad enough we have to scrap with that snobby bunch of save-the-canyon idiots and their national park hooey!"

"Put your brain in gear before you run your mouth, Haney!" Wendy shouted from behind Joe and Frank.

Gordo stood up beside his father and shouted back at Wendy. "Who wants big government sticking its nose into our business? The canyon's ours!" he bellowed.

A rancher stood up and turned to face the Haneys. "For those of you who don't know me, I'm Nick Krakowski of the Ranchers' Guild," he said smoothly, with a diplomat's ease. "I represent a lot of good, hardworking people in this room— our sheep and cattle ranchers. Now, I don't want our canyon to be a national park, but I don't want it turned into 'Vissenland' either. We have to keep the canyon in the state's hands. Right now my ranchers can graze their cattle for about two bucks an acre. You let these price controls get into the hands of a greedy jackal like Carl Vissen, and a lot of our ranchers are going to go bust. Then where will our local tax money come from?"

"Keep the land and the water pure! No grazing! No power boats!" Wendy shouted at Krakowski.

Lee Roy Samuels rose to his feet and yelled, "Those power boats bring a lot of tax dollars into this town, young lady."

"And into your pockets, Samuels," Wendy shouted back.

Mayor Latimer went to the mike as Vissen stepped back. "Folks, let's keep it down in here."

Frank was surprised to see Joe standing up. "If I may speak, I'm one of those river rats," Joe said. "I just want to say that my brother and I . . ."

Frank sank lower in his folding chair.

". . . came here only because Gehenna Canyon and Big Bison River are one of a kind. Unspoiled. Beautiful. Big Bison is one of the great rafting rivers. It seems to me all of you would want to keep it that way forever."

A chorus of voices answered Joe.

"What do you know?"

"Keep out of our business."

"Shut your trap, eco-freak!"

Joe looked flustered. "Hey, just because I care about the environment doesn't make me a—"

Mayor Latimer pounded the podium. "Everybody! Quiet down or I'll stop this meeting right now!"

"Whose pocket do you have your hands in this time, Latimer?" Lee Roy Samuels yelled at the mayor.

Artis joined in the yelling. "Are you going to sell our river to fat cat Vissen?"

Latimer turned bright red. "That's it! Town meeting over!" He turned off the microphone and stormed away from the platform. Frank watched Latimer shove his way through the crowd to get to the door. Vissen followed close behind him. Both Samuels and Artis blocked Latimer's way. "We're on the agenda," Samuels shouted. "You're not leaving till we've had our turn to speak!"

"Let me through," Latimer barked. "I said the meeting is *over*."

"No way," Gordo said, planting himself right in front of the mayor.

Frank watched Latimer try to push Gordo aside. Gordo fell against his father, then jumped back and took a swing at the mayor. In an instant Billy Two Trees was between the two, and the confrontation was over.

Frank joined Joe in following the crowd toward the door.

As the townspeople scattered into the twilight, Wendy caught up with Frank and Joe. "Guys, I need to talk to you tomorrow," she said. "But we'd better not meet out at Dad's camp. Whoever shot Dad might be watching. You never know what's lurking in those woods."

"Where, then?" Frank asked.

Wendy pointed to an old wood-frame office building two doors down from the town hall. "That's my mom's office. She shares a suite of offices with Nick Krakowski of the Ranchers' Guild. Let's meet there at ten."

By the time Joe and Frank reached their cabin, they were exhausted. Owen's camp was eerily quiet. The only sounds were the faint rushing of water and the chirp of crickets. Joe got out of the van first and headed for the door. Before he opened the lock with the keys Wendy had given them earlier, he turned to Frank.

"Bring a flashlight! There's something on our door!" Frank dashed over and lit up the cabin door with the flashlight from the van.

Nailed to the door were a pair of plastic soldier action figures. The nails punctured the torsos of the figures, which were dripping with red paint. Below the gruesome figures hung a crudely lettered warning tag. It read Enviro-Freaks Will Die.

Chapter
6

AT TEN O'CLOCK the next morning, Joe and Frank turned the corner onto Main Street in Gehenna and saw Wendy and Gordo standing on the porch of the Ranchers' Guild office, where Wendy's mother worked. Frank carried a paper bag.

As they approached, Gordo said, "Look, Wendy, I just wanted you to know that I had nothing to do with shooting your dad." Gordo looked upset.

"Who did shoot him, then?" Joe asked as he stepped onto the porch.

"My dad doesn't know anything about guns," Gordo said defiantly. "He doesn't even *own* a gun. When Owen Watson was shot, Dad was on his cellular phone making a call. I can prove it." Joe thought that Gordo was a little too defensive.

Frank almost said something, then decided to keep his mouth shut. He remembered Artis telling them at his dealership that his motor had failed. Who had he been calling? Frank wondered.

"Look, Gordo, I just told the police what I saw. Nobody's trying to point a finger at your father," Joe said calmly. "He just happened to be on the river yesterday morning, and we didn't know where he was when the shot was fired."

Gordo stood very close to Joe. "My dad is not a killer," he said quietly but intensely.

"I think you'd better leave, Gordo," Wendy said firmly.

"You and Nature Boy got a date?" Gordo sneered.

"Lay off it, Haney," Joe said. "We're just here to talk."

"C'mon, Nature Boy," Gordo said. "Show me how you're going to save the planet. You going to get a bunch of your friends to come hug the trees with you?"

Joe stood very still, trying to control his anger. He knew Gordo was just trying to provoke him. Gordo stood eye to eye with him, but Joe stayed cool and stared him down. Gordo looked away, but then shoved Joe in the shoulder.

In a flash Frank leaped between the two. With a few quick moves Frank had Gordo Haney's arms pinned behind his back. Gordo was caught completely off guard and dropped to his knees.

"Hey, man," Gordo gasped. "I wasn't going to

hurt him. Let me go." Frank released Gordo, who stood up and backed away from him, holding his palms in front of him.

"How'd you do that?" Gordo asked.

Joe broke a smile. "Frank's full of surprises— like having a black belt in karate."

Gordo backed a little farther away, nodding. "Cool," he said, trying to regain his composure. "I gotta learn some of that stuff."

Frank leaned over to pick up the paper bag he had dropped, while Gordo turned on his heel and strode away swiftly.

"Thanks, bro," Joe said casually.

Wendy watched Gordo get into his blue pickup truck and drive away. "I've never seen Gordo like this," she said, with a note of bewilderment. "He's really changed since we broke up. I mean, he could be a real dweeb now and then, but he's basically a really nice guy. Now it's like he's scared of something."

Joe took a deep breath and said, "Maybe he's scared of someone finding out the truth."

Wendy walked into her mother's office with Joe and Frank in tow. "Got to use the conference room, Mom," Wendy said to her mother, who sat at an old wooden rolltop desk, tapping the keyboard of a laptop computer.

"Aren't you going to introduce me to your friends?" the woman asked.

"Oh, Mom . . ." Wendy said, rolling her eyes.

Frank and Joe both walked over to the desk and introduced themselves.

The woman stood up. "I'm Doreen Falk-Watson," she said as she shook hands firmly.

"We're sorry about what happened to your husband," Frank said.

Doreen sighed and said in a matter-of-fact way, "I'm not surprised that he's in this kind of trouble. And, FYI, Owen hasn't been my husband for a couple of years now. I've kept his last name tacked onto mine because it's cheaper than getting new business cards printed," Doreen said wryly. She turned to Wendy. "I hope you're not using the conference room to plot the revolution like your father."

"Mom, we just need to talk, okay?" Wendy headed toward the conference room in the back.

Doreen scowled. "I don't want to have to explain anything to Nick." She stood up and followed her daughter.

"Nick?" Joe asked.

Doreen turned back toward Frank and Joe and said, "Nick Krakowski. He was at the town meeting last night. He and I work together for the Ranchers' Guild."

Wendy sat at a round oak table in the conference room. "Mom, the sooner you leave us alone, the sooner we can get out of your office," she said.

Frank was never one to let a trail go unexplored. "Why weren't you surprised that Mr. Watson was shot?" he asked Doreen.

Doreen took a deep breath. "Owen and I used to work together years ago. Back then I was as passionate about saving that canyon as he still is. We gathered a lot of evidence on all sides of the issue—things that could put some people in jail. I warned Owen to be careful, but Owen doesn't know the meaning of the word 'compromise.' He's stepped on a lot of toes in this town, some of them pretty hard."

"What made you join the other side?" Joe asked.

Doreen chuckled. "I suppose I still feel the same way deep down inside as I ever did. I care about the river and the land, but ideals don't always pay the bills. Neither does Owen. He's never been quite able to scrape together the alimony or child support payments. So my own principles follow my bank account."

"Mom won't take Dad to court to collect," Wendy chimed in. "Imagine that? A lawyer who won't sue."

"I know that Owen puts every spare dollar back into the Save the Canyon Foundation," Doreen said. "I can't bring myself to pull the rug out from under him. Besides, the Ranchers' Guild is far from being the enemy. The impact grazing has on the environment is nothing compared to what could happen if someone else got their hands on the canyon. I think our group could cooperate with Owen if he'd only listen to reason."

"*Okay*, Mom," Wendy said impatiently.

Doreen shook her head and walked back to her desk. She spotted the paper bag Frank carried. "What's that?" she asked.

"It's our breakfast. Some doughnuts," Frank said, thinking quickly.

"That's what I thought," Doreen said. "Please don't eat in the conference room, okay?"

Wendy shut the door. Frank put the bag in front of him and pulled out the action figures and the note. "We found a little present on our door last night."

Wendy gasped when she saw the soldiers splattered with red paint. "Who did that?"

"That's what we'd like to know," Frank said.

"Do you think it was Gordo or Artis Haney?" Joe asked Wendy.

"It could have been anybody," Wendy said. "Mom's right . . . Dad has a lot of enemies in this area. You saw most of them at the meeting last night."

"I understand," Frank said. "But why threaten us?"

"That's why I wanted to talk to you guys," Wendy said. "Mom doesn't like it that I work with Dad, but she can't stop me. There's a lot of stuff Dad knows that he's never told anybody. But I know enough to tell you two that this is dangerous."

"Don't worry about us," Frank said.

"We can handle it," Joe added.

"What I'm trying to say is . . ." Wendy looked at the door and went on. "I'm going to keep fighting Dad's war while he's in the hospital. I don't want you guys to get caught in the cross fire. Maybe it would be better if you just left town. I mean, for your own good."

"No way," Joe said.

"We're here to help," Frank said. "And we're not going to leave until we find out who tried to kill your father."

"You don't have to—" Wendy began.

"We're here for the duration," Joe said.

Wendy smiled and said a grateful "Thanks."

On their way out, Frank stopped again at Doreen's desk. "Thanks for letting us use your office," he said. "Just one more thing . . ."

"What's that?" Doreen smiled.

"Can you tell me where you and Mr. Krakowski stand with regard to Owen's plans to make the canyon a national park?"

"As the guild's lawyer," Doreen said firmly, "I can't reveal what our organization is doing or what associations we've made. Confidential. Attorney-client privilege it's called."

"I understand," Frank said.

As Frank turned to leave, Doreen called out, "I *can* offer you some advice, though. Ask Owen what he's got locked in his files."

Frank jumped into the driver's seat of the van, and Joe got in the passenger side. "Where are we headed now?" Joe asked.

"Gehenna Memorial," Frank said as he put the key in the ignition. "We've got to try to talk to Owen Watson."

As the engine turned over, there was a loud scraping and grinding noise. Frank leaned forward and saw a bright orange flash and a cloud of smoke.

"Get out of the van!" Frank shouted to Joe. "The engine's on fire!"

Chapter

7

JOE DOVE INTO THE BACK of the van and grabbed the fire extinguisher as Frank popped open the hood over the engine. Acrid smoke rose in a foul-smelling cloud. Two long blasts from the fire extinguisher, and the fire was out.

Frank leaned over and sniffed. "Electrical," he said.

"Look, Frank!" Joe exclaimed. He pointed to the ashes of a greasy paper towel wedged into the engine. "The starter set that on fire."

"And look at this," Frank said, pointing to the ground, where several more toy soldiers lay, this time melted into strange, twisted shapes.

"Another warning," Joe said.

* * *

"I'm going to have to keep your van here till I've checked it all out," Billy Two Trees said as he dusted the van for prints.

Thunder rumbled in the distance. Chief Two Trees looked up at the clouds. "Going to cut loose soon," he said. Chief Two Trees nodded at the plastic action figures that were lying on the pavement near the van. "Any guess who did all this to you?" he asked.

Frank was pacing in the parking lot. "Well, this morning we had a little run-in with Gordo."

"Join the club," the chief deadpanned. "That kid's just walking around going 'tick-tick-tick.' But he seems a little old to be playing with dolls."

Lightning flashed, followed a few seconds later by a clap of thunder. Chief Two Trees looked at the skies. "My old grandmother—a full-blood Blackfoot—always told me thunderstorms mean the sky is laughing at us . . . it sees things we'll never know," the chief said. "But then, she never believed that Neil Armstrong actually set foot on the moon. She swore it was trick photography on a Hollywood soundstage."

Chief Two Trees slammed the hood of the van and stooped down to pick up the plastic figurines. "Do me a favor, boys, just lie low in your cabin so that I can start to track down the sniper who shot Owen."

"Listen, Chief, we never expected anything like this to happen," Joe said.

The chief shrugged. *"Everybody's* ticking around here, not just Gordo Haney. My job is to try to figure where the next explosion is going to hit."

Nick Krakowski rushed across the parking lot. Chief Two Trees rose to his feet, standing almost a foot taller than Krakowski. "Now what?" the chief asked.

"I just got a call from one of my ranchers down in the canyon," Krakowski said. "He found a couple of his sheep dead in the pastures. Shot in the head and left to rot."

Nick seemed to suddenly recognize Frank and Joe. He asked, "Who are you two, and why were you in my office this morning?"

Frank and Joe exchanged quick looks. "How did you know we were in your office?" Joe asked.

"I was having my ham and eggs in the diner across the square," Nick said. "The waitress recognized you from the local TV news."

"The eyes of Gehenna are upon you," Chief Two Trees joked to Joe and Frank. "Claire knows everything about everybody around these parts."

Suddenly it started to rain, a rough, pelting storm. "Let's all get in my four-by-four," the chief said, "I'll drop you two guys back at Watson's camp, then Nick and I will check out the sheep assassinations."

* * *

At noon Joe Hardy stood in the cabin, looking out through the screen door. Frank was lying on his bunk, dozing restlessly. Joe watched the rain splatter on the surface of Big Bison River and wished that he and his brother were out in a raft, as they had planned. In his head he ran over the events of the last twenty-four hours.

Out of the corner of his eye, Joe caught something moving on the cliff face on the other side of the river. The movement was as far downriver as Joe could see, almost out of sight. It looked as if a man had materialized out of nowhere.

Joe ran to his suitcase and fetched a pair of binoculars. Focusing on where he had noticed movement, he saw a figure in a green, camouflage-patterned rain parka clambering up a narrow path in the cliff wall, then disappearing over the ridge at the top of the cliff.

Joe flung the screen door open and ran down to the riverbank to get a better look, but the figure had vanished. Frank, awakened by the door slamming, came out of the cabin and joined Joe. Joe handed him the binoculars.

"Halfway up the cliff. Follow the footpath. There's a cave entrance," Joe whispered. "You can barely see it behind those bushes."

Frank nodded. "I see it."

The two brothers looked at each other. Without saying a word, they ran back to Owen's cabin to get into life jackets.

Fifteen minutes later Joe and Frank were once

again in a raft on Big Bison River. Because of the hard, driving rain, the river flowed more swiftly than it had the day before. In a matter of seconds they reached the point where Joe had spotted the man.

They beached the raft and scrambled up the side of the cliff. The footpath that led to the cave entrance was slippery because of all the rain. Joe and Frank carefully crawled up the slick, muddy path, grasping the branches of the scrubby bushes that grew on the bank.

Frank had to double over to squeeze through the narrow mouth of the tiny cave. Inside he switched on his flashlight, then stuck his head and right arm out of the cave. "Come on in," Frank said to Joe, offering his hand to steady his brother.

Joe inched toward the cave's mouth carefully, then wedged himself inside. The damp cave walls gave off a musty smell. From what Frank and Joe could see in the flashlight beam, the cave was just a small, closed chamber.

Frank flashed the light around and saw six long wooden crates against the back of the low chamber.

Joe crept toward them and tried to lift one. "They're heavy," he whispered.

Frank scanned the nearest crate with his light. "Look, Joe!" he exclaimed. "The bottom is covered with fresh mud. They've been dragged in here since the rain started."

"Dragged, not carried," Joe said.

"Meaning . . . ?" Frank asked.

"One person," Joe said. "Two or more would have carried. One person would drag."

"Right," Frank said. "But what's in them?"

"Only one way to find out," Joe said.

"I know that," Frank said, turning and shining the flashlight beam in Joe's eyes. "So why don't you open one?"

Joe shielded his eyes with his hands. "Because my dorky brother is shining his high beam in my eyes, and I can't see anything."

"Sorry." Frank turned the beam back toward the boxes. "Wait a minute. Whoever put them here will be suspicious if they're opened."

Frank and Joe looked over the rest of the boxes and found that only the nearest box had fresh mud on it. The rest were caked with dried mud. Joe knocked on the other five boxes. They rang hollow.

"I get it," Frank said softly. "This is a drop-off point. For some reason, one person drags these crates down here, then someone else empties them."

"Okay, I'll buy that," Joe said. "But why?"

Frank thought a moment. "If we look inside the full crate, maybe we'll know."

"That's what I said," Joe huffed. He moved closer to the crates. "Frank, I'll try to pry up one of the slats. Shine the light in. We can hammer it back with a rock."

Using the all-purpose Swiss Army knife he was carrying, Joe carefully pried up one of the crate's slats, just enough to see inside.

As he peered into the box, Joe whistled softly, then leaned back so that Frank could have a look.

"Guns," Frank whispered.

Outside the cave, the rain continued to pelt down in torrents. Even though the path was slick and muddy, Frank and Joe made it to the top of the cliff in seconds. About thirty feet back from the edge, Joe spotted fresh tire tracks. He motioned Frank over.

"Looks like a four-by-four to me," Frank said.

"Yeah, you're right. What else could make it up here without a road?"

"Come on," Frank said. "Let's trace it."

Joe and Frank followed the tracks across an open pasture and through a thick stand of trees. The heavy rain and slippery mud made the vehicle's route hard to follow.

"He must have driven off into the woods over there," Frank said as he pointed toward a shadowy stand of pines.

Through the trees in the distance, Joe spotted the taillights of a gray 4 × 4 truck. "There he is!" Joe exclaimed.

Joe and Frank ran into the edge of the woods, slipping and sloshing through the mud. The taillights vanished between the trees.

"We can't run fast enough to catch him," Joe said.

"No," Frank said. "But Big Bison River can."

Frank and Joe turned back toward the riverbank, then heard a deep growl. Frank looked up and froze in his tracks.

Above them on a high rock crouched a sleek, angry mountain lion, its fangs bared. It tensed, ready to attack.

"Don't move," Frank said softly, grabbing Joe's jacket.

With a loud snarl, the mountain lion leaped through the air . . . straight at Frank.

Chapter

8

AS THE MOUNTAIN LION SPRANG, Frank ducked to his left. The beast hit the ground on all four paws, then spun around and snarled.

Just as Frank was about to turn and make a run for it, a loud shotgun blast burst through the pattering of the hard-driving rain. The mountain lion flinched and ran into the woods.

"Someone knows we're here," Joe said.

"Run for the raft!" Frank yelled. He and Joe ran, slid, and tumbled down the muddy slope of the bank and splashed into the icy water of the Big Bison. Quickly they pulled the raft from the bank and leaped into it.

"Paddle!" Frank shouted to Joe.

The river's swift current swept the Hardys toward the rapids where they had spilled the day before.

"Keep us to starboard," Joe called. This time Joe and Frank expertly guided the raft through the huge boulders of the narrow pass. The swirling waters thrust them forward through a deep, rocky gorge.

Very soon the river widened again, and the current slowed down. Frank and Joe stopped paddling and turned to look back. "I think we're safe . . . for the time being," Frank said.

Joe turned his gaze up to the high banks. "Look!" he exclaimed, pointing a finger to a clearing ahead in the woods. There, half hidden behind trees and brush, were a group of crude wooden shacks around a large stone campfire circle.

Joe and Frank saw the same gray 4 × 4 truck pull up to the largest building and stop. Quickly and silently the Hardys steered the raft to the riverbank and beached it. Moving as stealthily as they could, they climbed out of the raft and crept up the bank toward the buildings.

As they drew nearer, Joe and Frank noticed that a blue pickup was parked next to the gray 4 × 4.

"Haney!" Frank whispered.

"Father or son?" Joe responded.

The door of the building stood open. Frank and Joe dropped to the ground, which was thick with damp, sticky leaves and pine needles. They could just barely see inside the shack.

"It's *Artis* Haney," Frank said softly.

"Who's the other one?" Joe asked. Another man paced the dirt floor inside the shack, wearing the camouflage rain gear Joe had seen through the binoculars.

From the restless way the two men circled each other, Frank could tell they were having a tense discussion. "I can't see well enough," Frank said. "Let's get closer."

Frank started to crawl slowly in the direction of the vehicles, Joe right behind him. Frank turned back to his brother and whispered, "If we get behind the gray truck, we can see both of them at the same time."

"As long as they both can't see us," Joe said.

Joe and Frank huddled on the driver's side of the gray 4 × 4, where they could see both men clearly. Haney wore a rubber raincoat. The other man had on a ski mask under the hood of his poncho.

Joe leaned over to Frank and whispered, "I wish we could hear what they were saying." Joe pressed heavily on Frank's back and strained to get as close as he could without being obvious.

"Get off my back," Frank whispered. Joe backed up slightly, straightening up as he did so.

Frank heard a dull thud, followed by a half-voiced "Ow." He looked around and saw that Joe had bumped his head on the side-view mirror of the vehicle.

Frank's eyes darted back to the open door of the building. Both men were standing in the door frame, looking out at their vehicles. Frank reached behind himself and yanked Joe to the ground. It was too late. They'd been spotted.

"Hey, somebody's out there," Artis Haney said. Both men started walking toward Joe and Frank.

Frank leaped to his feet and opened the door of the 4 × 4. He pulled Joe up and shoved him across the front seat, then jumped behind the wheel.

"Yes!" Frank said, finding the key still in the ignition. Both men started running when they heard Frank start the engine. He jammed the vehicle into reverse and floored it.

"Come back here!" Frank heard the man in the ski mask yell. But Frank had other plans. He shifted into gear and barreled through the woods toward a gravel road.

He glanced over at Joe, who had turned completely around in the passenger seat and was staring at the back of the vehicle.

"Jackpot!" Joe shouted. "There are enough guns and bullets in here for a small army."

"You realize auto theft is a felony, right?" Billy Two Trees said sternly as he paced in his office. Joe Hardy opened his mouth to speak, but the chief continued without giving him a chance to say anything. "On the other hand, dealing in unlicensed, unregistered, unnumbered semiautomatic weapons is also a felony." He paused and shook his head. "You guys brought me a truckful of illegal weapons—without even meaning to. *That's* quite a feat," Chief Two Trees said.

"Does that mean you're not charging us?" Frank asked in all seriousness. There was a very long pause as the chief stared into space.

"I'll think it over," Chief Two Trees said at last. "While I'm thinking, let's check the plates on that gray four-by-four." The chief rolled the office chair away from his desk and over to a computer terminal. He quickly punched in a series of numbers. While waiting, he leaned back in his chair and hummed a few bars of a tuneless song, never taking his eyes off Frank and Joe.

"What are those buildings out in the woods?" Joe asked.

"That used to be an old hunting camp," Billy said. "It became state land, but the forest service has let it get run down. A couple of years ago some of the businessmen in town got a little money together and fixed it up. They used it to hunt and fish there, or so I thought. Now it looks as though the Knights of Liberty may be using it for some kind of gunrunning operation."

"Shouldn't you investigate?" Frank asked.

"By *myself?*" the chief asked. "In case you haven't noticed, I'm a one-man police force. Till now all I had to do was find out who shot Owen Watson, who stole Wendy's video, who left you guys that little present on your door, who rigged your van engine, who slaughtered those sheep, then maybe file grand theft auto charges against you two. Oh, and break up the fistfights at our town meetings. No, sir, this little truckload you uncovered is a matter for the Feds—the Bureau of Alcohol, Tobacco and Firearms, maybe even the FBI."

The computer beeped. Chief Two Trees spun around in his chair and looked at the screen. "Gentlemen, according to the Montana Bureau of Motor Vehicles, you have stolen a rental . . . which is registered to a car dealer in Gehenna named Artis Haney. If you'd care to leave it in my custody, I could see my way to returning that van of yours."

"Does that mean we can go?" Joe asked eagerly.

The chief smiled at Joe and Frank. "I doubt Artis Haney will want to press charges against you, unless he's prepared to answer to me about those weapons. I'd say for now you're a couple of free men."

Joe and Frank wasted no time leaving the chief's office. In the Gehenna municipal parking lot Frank and Joe headed toward their black van.

"Joe! Frank!" came a shout from the direction of Main Street.

"Check this out," Wendy said, dashing over to the two. "Carl Vissen's pushed up the date of the special town meeting because of the stuff that's been going on. He thinks that the sooner he makes his presentation, the sooner things will quiet down."

"You don't know half of what's going on," Joe said. Quickly he and Frank briefed Wendy about their discoveries.

"A lot of funny stuff has been happening around here," Wendy said. "I've got to ask Dad about it, as soon as I can get back in to see him. They won't put any phone calls through to him, and visiting hours aren't till later tonight."

"What about this town meeting with Vissen?" Joe asked.

"I've heard that he's planned a big video presentation tomorrow night in the town hall," Wendy said. "The town's charter says that anyone can make a speech or presentation at any public meeting, as long as they're on the agenda. Mom and Nick have used that loophole a lot. Dad, too."

Frank asked, "What does that mean for us?"

Wendy smiled coyly. "I'm planning a little video presentation of my own, and I might need you guys to help. I'll give you all the details later. But there's one hitch: We have to petition the mayor to get on the agenda."

The burnished, walnut-paneled walls of Mayor Latimer's office were covered with all kinds of stuffed and mounted wild animals, from birds and squirrels to a gigantic moose's head. Joe, Frank, and Wendy sat in smooth leather armchairs waiting for Latimer to get off the telephone.

"I don't think we should bring up any animal rights issues with this guy," Joe whispered to Wendy.

Latimer hung up the phone and smiled a too cheery politician's smile at Wendy. "So what is it I can do for you and your friends, Ms. Watson?"

Quickly Wendy explained that she wanted a slot on the meeting's agenda. The mayor grinned again, in the same patronizing way, but the expression in his eyes was anything but cheerful.

"I'm afraid I can't do that," Latimer said. "You see, Wendy, I hold you and your friends partially responsible for disrupting last night's regular meeting."

"But—" Wendy blurted as Latimer cut her off.

"And your friends here aren't even residents. I can't be giving time in our town meetings to *strangers,* Wendy. You have to understand that."

"I realize we've only been here a couple of days," Frank said. "But we've received a pretty good introduction to the local issues."

Latimer stopped smiling. "Look, son, I'll level with you," he said. "There are state issues and local issues. A lot of the state regulations about the use of the canyon are soon to be rewritten. That's what everyone's so hung up about."

Latimer had begun to perspire. He continued, "I can't get involved on anything but the local level. Some very bizarre things have happened in the last couple of days, but I think its the work of some fringe lunatic who's gone off the deep end. There is certainly no kind of organized— what's the word?—paramilitary group at work here. You know, a bunch of vigilantes or some such thing."

Frank and Joe looked at each other. They wondered why Latimer looked so fearful.

Latimer's telephone buzzed. He picked it up, listened for a moment, then said, "Send him in."

Carl Vissen stepped into the mayor's office. Latimer made introductions all around, but Wendy refused to acknowledge the well-dressed, silver-haired developer.

Carl Vissen looked at Wendy with what seemed to be genuine concern. "I'm sorry about what happened to your father," he said. "We've had our differences over the years, but he's a good, honest man."

Wendy looked as if she was going to explode. "How would you know what an honest man is?" Wendy shouted, and stormed out of the mayor's office.

Latimer and Vissen looked at Frank and Joe. Frank felt awkward. Joe didn't know whether to follow Wendy or stay. He and Frank suddenly felt like the strangers they were in the small town.

"I can only imagine what she's feeling," Vissen said. "It was a shock to all of us. I'm sure you two young men were upset, too." He turned to

Latimer. "George, maybe we can set these fine fellows straight on a few little matters."

Vissen perched on the front of the mayor's desk and spoke with a well-practiced warmth and familiarity. "A lot of people in these parts would like to make a villain out of me, just because I'm successful. Well, I can't help that. And if the resorts I build and develop bring a lot of people into a beautiful area like this, I'm as aware as Owen Watson that the natural resources can take a beating. True, George?" Vissen turned to the mayor.

"True, Carl," Mayor Latimer said, his head bobbing up and down.

"It's easy to imagine that I'll just bring in the bulldozers and ruin things, but that's ridiculous," Vissen said. "Without this beautiful canyon and river, who would want to come to a Carl Vissen resort? Let me tell you, my plans for developing this area will please everyone who doesn't have some ax to grind."

"Fellows," the mayor said, standing up, "Carl and I have to discuss the agenda for tomorrow night's meeting. I'm truly sorry about the way things have gone for you, and I hope you'll come back to our little town soon." With that, Latimer ushered the Hardys to the door.

The Hardys walked quickly from the mayor's office to the Gehenna Diner.

Joe scanned the diner before he and Frank sat

down in a well-worn booth. "If the locals are going to track our every move, we might as well be on display," he said to his brother.

"Joe, you're brilliant," Frank said.

"Of course, but what made you realize it just now?" Joe asked.

Claire, the waitress, came over to the table. She took down their order, handed it to the cook, and resumed her customary perch behind the counter, watching her little television and gabbing on the phone.

"Everyone's been telling us to get lost or lie low. If we want to find out who's behind the shooting and all of this gunrunning, we should just do the opposite," Frank said softly.

Joe was puzzled. "What do you mean? Walk around with targets on our backs?"

"Listen. Nobody wants us to go back out on the river. Obviously we're too close to somebody's secret operation. Wendy's a qualified river raft guide. We're going back on the river."

Joe nodded, then said, "We'll need some kind of cover, and I don't think we can ask Billy Two Trees. What about Ranger MacKendrick? Maybe he could keep us in sight from a safe distance."

Frank thought it over. "If we explain to him what we've discovered, he might go for it. Let's drop in on him after lunch."

After finishing their meal, the Hardy's asked Claire for directions to the forest service's ranger station. It was on the outskirts of town, a low concrete-block building with a big garage behind it. The building was painted the same forest green as the pickup truck parked near the garage.

"Looks like MacKendrick's there," Joe remarked as they pulled up to the station.

As they walked to the front door, Joe grabbed Frank's shoulder. "The window," he said, pointing to an obvious bullet hole in the plate glass window to the right of the door. Around it, the glass had cracked into a splintered spider's web. Slivers of glass covered the ground.

The front door was ajar. Frank and Joe entered cautiously. MacKendrick lurched forward, clutching his bleeding bicep, and toppled into Joe's arms.

Chapter
9

THE SAME SHORT, DARK-HAIRED DOCTOR who had operated on Owen Watson tended to Ranger MacKendrick's wound. "It's a good thing you found Roger," the doctor told Frank and Joe as he finished taping a bandage over the ranger's upper arm. Roger winced.

"Keep still," the doctor said. "That's a nasty wound, Roger. Looks as much like a burn as a bullet hole."

"Who's in charge of patrolling the river if you're not there?" Joe asked Roger. "Do you have a deputy or something?"

Roger chuckled. "I wish I did. Then I could turn over all the paperwork and spend more time out of the office, doing my *real* job," he said.

The doctor stepped over to a cabinet and pulled out a sling for the ranger's arm.

"Are you right-handed, Roger?" the doctor asked.

"I'm a lefty," Roger replied.

"Good thing, then," the doctor said, putting the sling on Roger's wounded right arm. "You can keep up with your pencil pushing."

"Does that mean I can go?" Roger asked, trying to get up from the examining table.

"Hold on there," the doctor barked. "You shouldn't drive with the kind of painkillers I've given you. Why don't you just stay here till my shift's over? I'll drop you at home."

"We can drive him back," Joe offered, standing up.

Roger waved a hand at Joe. "That's all right," he said. "You and your brother have done enough for one day."

Back at Watson's camp, Frank and Joe pulled the raft out of Owen's cabin and got it ready for the river. Wendy sat at a table, arranging her video equipment.

"We'll put in downriver, by that old hunting camp," Wendy said. "The Knights of Liberty may expect you to come back around there."

"What could happen if we're caught on the river at night?" Frank asked Wendy.

Wendy looked up as she loaded a videotape into her camera. "We could get busted or fined.

And Dad *could* get his river rights suspended, since we're technically using his permit."

"I don't think Roger will be out patrolling the river anyway," Joe said. "He'll probably be home sleeping off his painkillers."

"Can that camera record in the dark?" Frank asked.

Wendy smiled. "This baby can pick up things in really low light," she said. "You never know what kind of water monster is going to turn up out there."

Frank strapped himself into an orange life jacket, as did Joe. "If our idea works, whoever shot your father will come after us," Frank said to Wendy. "I think we can assume our gunman wanted Roger out of the way, too."

"Right," Joe said. "If someone's running guns on the river, that would explain why he wanted Owen and Roger out of his path. But now we'll be in the way, too."

Wendy zipped her camera bag shut, then looked at Joe and Frank. "I know I asked you to steer clear of all this mess, and I meant it. But now that you're in this deep, I want you to know that it really means a lot to both me and my dad."

Frank's eyes narrowed. "Joe and I couldn't go back to Bayport now, knowing the guy who shot your dad is still on the loose."

Joe grinned. "Besides, we came out to ride the

rapids. If we don't, we'll feel really ripped off. So, let's get going!"

As they eased the raft into the water and jumped aboard, the three floaters listened carefully for the sound of river jet motors. Not a man-made sound could be heard as the dwindling sunlight sparkled on the water.

With Frank and Joe paddling in the front of the raft, the three floaters cleared the first pass smoothly. Joe remarked to the others that it seemed like a long time ago that they'd had their first clash with the Haneys at that same pass.

The current pulled them gently along. Wendy took her camera from the waterproof bag. She pointed the camera at Joe and Frank and told them to state their names, the date, and the time.

"We need a point of reference," she said. Then she handed Joe the camera and asked him to take a shot of her as well.

As Joe paddled, Frank asked Wendy, "What's this video project you were talking about?"

Wendy sighed. "I was going to put together a tape of all the violations and destruction that have happened to the river and the canyon since the laws were loosened up. If people can see the effects of what they're doing, it might change their minds. But if I can't get a time slot at the meeting, there's no point. It looks as though Carl Vissen and the mayor are thick as thieves."

"What's the story on Vissen?" Joe asked.

Wendy put up her hand and watched the river.

"Later," she said. "We're coming up on Niagara Junior."

"Niagara Junior?" Joe chuckled.

"When I was a kid, Dad and I gave all the rapids nicknames. Now Dad uses them all the time." Joe could tell Wendy shared a lot of good memories with her father and that she was missing him.

Wendy stuck the video camera into her camera bag and zipped it closed as the current sped up. She became tense and efficient. "Sit in the back, Joe and Frank, and use your paddles like rudders. Let the current carry us along."

Everyone scrambled into position. "Okay," Wendy shouted over the growing sound of the rushing waters. "Take us left."

The raft gained more speed as the Hardys did what Wendy had told them.

"Quick, turn to the right!" Wendy yelled. Frank and Joe saw a huge boulder looming to their left. The raft swerved and nearly scraped along the boulder's side. After that the river looked calm for a moment.

"We're going to make three drops in a row really soon," Wendy said. "Keep your paddles clear, sit still, and ride out the first one. Then get the paddles back and turn us fast to the left. Sharp turn and hold on. The drop hits you without warning."

Way off in the distance, Frank thought he heard a river jet engine. Joe and Wendy heard it, too. Whatever it was, it was going downstream a lot faster than the raft.

Wendy continued. "You'll get only a second to catch your breath before Niagara Junior, the third drop. It's shaped like a horseshoe. We have to go right down the middle or the right. *Not* to the left. Before we hit Junior, move to the front of the raft. We need your weight in front. Got all that?"

"Got it!" Frank and Joe shouted back with one voice.

The first white water came up faster than Frank and Joe expected. Suddenly they felt as if the river had dropped out from underneath them. They were in the air. Frank and Joe held tight to the ropes that ran along the sides of the raft.

The raft hit the water a second later, sounding like somebody smacking a hand on a slab of marble. Joe and Frank whooped as they hit.

"All right!" Joe yelled.

"Paddles!" Wendy shouted.

Frank and Joe used their paddles to turn the raft quickly to the left.

"Harder!" Wendy called out. They swung the raft even sharper. The water around them churned and foamed. The rubber raft skidded and thumped over the low rocks. One bump sent Wendy's camera bag in the air, but Joe caught it and jammed it between his feet.

One second the river stretched in front of them. The next, it disappeared from sight.

Wendy, Joe, and Frank leaned back and held their breaths as the raft plummeted almost straight down the steep rapids.

The front of the raft crashed into the spray and foam at the bottom. A bright white wall of water flew up over the raft, soaking the three river rats. In a second they were past the rapids.

"Wow!" Frank yelled as he shook the water from his brown hair. "That was intense!"

"Amazing!" Joe said.

"You ain't seen nothin' yet!" Wendy called out. "Get in the front now," she hollered.

Frank and Joe flung themselves forward in the raft. About a hundred yards ahead loomed what Wendy called Niagara Junior. It was like the real Niagara Falls in miniature—a horseshoe-shaped gouge in the river beyond which only air appeared.

"Guide us straight down the middle!" Wendy yelled, her eyes glued to the river ahead.

Suddenly the loud crack of a gunshot thundered over the roar of the cascading water and ricocheted between the cliffs. Three pairs of eyes looked up.

Frank spotted the man first in the fading light. "It's him!" he shouted. "The sniper!"

Standing on the cliff high above the river, on the right side of the boat, was a man dressed in camouflage, wearing a ski mask. In his left hand he held a carbine rifle. He had fired a shot into the air to distract the rafters.

Wendy looked back at the river. "Get us to the center!"

Joe and Frank looked ahead. The current had pulled them to the left side of the white water.

"Get us back to center!" Wendy cried again.

Frank and Joe paddled furiously, but the current had the raft and wouldn't let go.

Frank threw a quick look back at the sniper. He was gone.

Then Wendy screamed.

Wedged between the rocks lining the ridge of Niagara Junior were sharp, jagged saw blades.

The raft spun sideways in the current. There was a sickening ripping sound, and the raft almost exploded as the saw blades tore through its thick, rubbery skin.

Joe felt himself fly out of the boat and over the rapids. As he tried to look behind him, his own paddle, flung like a javelin by the mighty force of the water, struck him hard on the forehead. The pressure of the crashing water sucked him under. Joe blacked out as he smacked on the rocks at the bottom of the falls.

Chapter

10

THE WATER SHOOK JOE HARDY awake as it tossed him around under the falls. He felt a pair of arms thrust under his own. The next thing he knew, his head was above the surface of the water and he was gasping for air. His life jacket had helped keep him near the surface, where Frank could grab him.

The water drove them toward the bank. Ahead, Joe could see Wendy pulling herself out of the current and onto land. Frank hauled Joe out of the water, and they both collapsed on the bank, taking in gulps of air.

"I thought we'd lost you," Wendy said, trying to catch her breath.

"I saw that paddle coming straight at me," Joe gasped.

"Good thing it hit you in the head," Frank joked. "It couldn't hurt you there."

Joe shook the water from his ears. "Everybody's a comedian," he said.

"Seriously, are you okay?" Frank asked.

"Yeah, I'm a little soggy, but . . ." Joe winced as he tried to stand up. He thought that he might have pulled a muscle in his back, but he wouldn't admit it in front of Wendy.

"I think we've all been knocked around," Wendy said, examining the scrapes and bruises on her arms and legs. "It could have been worse."

Frank looked back at the top of the rapids. "We could have ended up like that."

The remains of the raft were hanging in shreds from the menacing saw blades.

"Well, bro, it worked," Joe said to Frank.

"What worked?"

"Your brilliant plan to get back on the river and draw the sniper out of hiding. A huge success, unless you're a raft."

"Should we go up there and get it?" Wendy asked.

"We'll have to come back for it some other time," Frank said. "Whoever set that trap for us is still out here."

"I'm sure he knows we didn't drown," Joe said, rubbing the knot on his head.

"Who?" Wendy asked.

"That guy Frank saw wearing camouflage and

a ski mask," Joe said. "We saw him with Haney at that hunting camp. We, uh, kind of took his four-by-four for a little test drive."

"You two guys aren't the center of attention all the time, you know," Wendy said. "I think that trap was set for *any* floaters who might have come by."

"Yeah," Joe said. "But we *did* stumble onto their cache of weapons in that little cave."

"Joe's right," Frank added, looking back at the shredded raft. "It doesn't look like anybody else has gone over those saw blades before."

"The first step was getting Ranger MacKendrick out of the way," Joe said.

"What does that mean?" Wendy asked. Joe and Frank both looked at her glumly. "You mean we're next?"

"Could be," Frank said tersely. "One thing I know, we're not safe out here on the banks. Let's head for higher ground."

Frank, Joe, and Wendy clambered up the sloping side of a bluff, then stood on the top overlooking the river. Frank peered into the deepening twilight.

"What are you looking for, Frank?" Wendy asked.

"Anything," Frank grunted. "Tire tracks, broken branches, fresh footprints in the mud. In a few minutes it'll be dark. We won't be able to find any clues our elusive friend might have left behind."

Wendy looked back and forth between Joe and Frank. "You guys are really serious about this."

Joe frowned. "Whoever shot your dad and tried to drown us is playing for keeps."

A distant roar made Joe turn and look upriver. "Listen!" he hissed. "River jets!"

"Get down!" Frank barked. Frank and Joe dropped onto their stomachs. Joe turned and grabbed Wendy's hand and pulled her to the ground.

"What's going on?" Wendy whispered.

"Don't let them see us!" Joe whispered back.

"It might be dark enough that they won't be able to," Wendy said.

Two men on river jets came soaring through the foam of the rapids at the center of Niagara Junior. They hooted and whooped as they hit the churning water at the bottom. Plumes of water sprayed from the sterns of their yellow-hulled, jet-powered watercrafts.

Wendy started to get up. Joe pulled her back down.

"What are you doing?" Joe said.

"Getting my camera out," Wendy answered.

"Stay down!" Frank said.

Wendy snorted, then crawled down the bluff to where she'd left the camera, slipping it from the waterproof bag. She followed the boaters down the river until they were out of sight, then trained her camera back on the wounded raft.

"Wendy, did you recognize those guys?" Joe asked.

"One of them looked kind of familiar," she said.

Joe noted that both men wore the same kind of hunter's camouflage that the man at the rapids had worn.

Wendy stopped the camera. "Listen!" she said. They all stood still. It was suddenly and eerily quiet. "They've stopped their engines."

Stealthily Wendy and the brothers moved along the bluff, following the winding course of the river. They stopped at a sharp bend. On the broad, sandy bank of the river, the two boaters had pulled up onshore. One of them was loading a shotgun. The other man held a large floodlight and also had a shotgun under his arm.

"What are they doing?" Frank asked.

"I don't know," Wendy said. "But I think I should get this on tape."

Wendy readied her camera as the second man switched on the floodlight, lighting the area around the boaters and plunging the rest of the river into an even darker gloom. The two men stood quietly and waited, muttering softly to each other in low voices that didn't carry up to the bluffs where Wendy, Frank, and Joe watched.

Wendy checked through the eyepiece of her

video camera. "At least they've given me plenty of light," she whispered to Frank and Joe.

The second man flashed the light up into the sky and around the sharp edges of the stone bluffs.

"Hit the ground!" Frank said as the lights swung around into his eyes. Joe and Wendy dropped to the ground again, holding their breaths.

"There they are!" said the man who held a shotgun.

"Get 'em!" the other man said.

Frank, Joe, and Wendy clutched the sparse grass on the bluff. A loud shotgun blast shook the ground under them.

"You missed that one, Al," said the man with the floodlight, flashing the beam around in the air again. "Maybe you'd better take the light and let me shoot."

Joe raised his head, then quickly ducked down again as he heard another shot.

"Got that one!" came a voice from the river.

Joe looked up again. Something black spun in the air and dropped to the riverbank below. Circling wildly in the beam of the floodlight were a swarm of small black bats, their sleek, shiny wings flashing in the stark white shaft of light.

Joe tapped his brother and Wendy. They looked up and saw the bats swirling and swooping through the beams of light.

"They're shooting at the bats," Joe said softly.

"I can't believe it!" Wendy sighed.

Both of the men continued to fire their guns at the bats.

Frank said, "The lights are drawing insects. The bats must think they're at a banquet."

"Yeah," Joe replied. "Their last meal."

"This is really gross," Wendy said as she knelt on the bluff. "Dad and I can use this."

By now it was completely dark. A full moon had come out, casting a dim, misty glow along the river. The thick trees overhead cast deep, dense shadows over the bluffs.

Frank turned to Joe. "I don't think either of these guys is the sniper."

"No," Joe said softly. "Just a bunch of cruel yahoos who think they're hotshots because they can blow away some bats."

"Let's keep moving," Frank said.

"I want to stay here a minute," Wendy said. "You guys go on ahead. I'll catch up."

Joe looked at Frank, then back at Wendy. "Are you sure you'll be okay?"

Wendy stopped her camera and tossed a look full of scorn back at Joe and Frank. "I know every inch of this river," she said. "You guys are the ones to worry about. Be sure you don't get your behinds full of buckshot."

Joe and Frank followed the Big Bison around a sharp bend. The bluffs sloped down toward the river where it widened and the current slowed.

At the point of the bend was a stand of trees where Frank and Joe could see both up and down the river. The opposite bank consisted of broad, flat stones, which centuries of rushing water had sanded smooth.

A rough dirt road ran down to the bank on that side. Joe thought that the particular spot on the river would be a likely place to launch a boat. A car with a trailer could back down almost into the water.

Scanning his eyes across to the opposite bank, Frank spotted a large, dark form behind some distant trees. "Over there!" he said to his brother. "Looks like a truck."

"Where?" Joe asked.

Frank pointed to a clump of bushes at the edge of the woods. Through the dim moonlight Joe could see what looked like the front of a truck hidden behind the bushes.

Joe squinted, trying to make out details. Something moved near the front of the truck. "There's somebody leaning against the truck," he said to Frank.

Frank tried to focus his eyes on the shadowy truck. Just as Joe had said, a man's figure leaned against the front of the truck. It was hard to make out the figure at all, but Frank thought that the man wore a hunter's camouflage.

The Hardys stood completely still, their eyes riveted on the figure. He turned on a flashlight and shone it up the river and across the shore.

Then the man seemed to send a signal with the light, turning it off and on three times. He did this twice.

A second later Frank and Joe heard a sound that was all too familiar, the earsplitting engines of approaching river jets. From upstream came the two men who had been shooting bats. Joe and Frank ducked behind the cool trunks of the trees that stood on the bend.

The engines of the boats slowed, then stopped, as the two men eased onto the gentle slope of the riverbank. In the faint light of the full moon, Frank and Joe saw the man at the truck move stealthily down to the bank. He wore some kind of mask over his features.

"That's our man," Frank said in a low but intense voice. Joe looked carefully. Frank continued, "It's the same man we saw up at the rapids and meeting with Artis Haney . . . or at least it *could* be."

"How can you tell?" Joe asked. "You and I would look exactly the same in that getup. Anybody can buy a ski mask."

The two boaters bent over into the hulls of their boats, then stood up, both holding what looked to Joe and Frank like semiautomatic weapons. They handed them to the man in the mask.

Frank whispered to his brother, keeping his eyes fixed on the illegal transaction, "That's all the proof we need. They *are* running guns up and down the river, but why?"

"And who *are* these guys?" Joe asked.

The man in the ski mask picked up an armload of guns and carried them up to the truck.

"Where's Wendy when we need her?" Joe asked. "She should be taping this."

"Maybe she should tape *this!*" came a voice from behind Joe and Frank. They spun around to see the barrel of a carbine rifle pointing at them. Holding the gun was a man in a ski mask.

Chapter

11

CROUCHING LOW, FRANK swung his right leg in a wide, hooking arc, sweeping the sniper's feet out from under him. There was a sharp crack as the masked man squeezed the trigger. But the gun's barrel was pointed skyward as the man fell backward.

Frank heard a shout from the other riverbank. "Hey! Who's up there?"

One of the boaters grabbed his floodlight and flashed it right into Frank's eyes.

The masked man struggled to his knees, trying to grasp the stock of his rifle.

"Run!" Frank yelled to Joe.

"No!" Joe yelled back.

Joe hit the masked man with a flying tackle and knocked him back onto the ground. Joe landed on top of him and pinned him. The masked man tried to wriggle out of Joe's wrestling hold. He held tight to his rifle with one hand while the other hand gripped his knit ski mask.

The two boaters started their river jets and headed toward the bank where Joe and Frank struggled with the masked man. On the far riverbank, the truck's motor turned over.

"Frank!" Joe shouted. "Give me a hand!"

The river jets skidded to the bank, and the two boaters leaped out.

Joe and Frank grabbed the masked man by the arms and legs and flipped him over and into the river. There was a dull *thunk,* followed by a loud moan of pain as the masked man's shoulder struck a rock.

Frank and Joe heard the man thrashing and splashing in the river as they raced up the rocky bank. The man groaned in pain and swore angrily.

"Head back for camp!" Joe shouted at Frank.

Joe and Frank raced through the dark woods. In the distance, they heard the truck's wheels spin in the slippery mud of the dirt road. Finally the truck caught some traction and sped off into the night. Behind them they could still faintly hear the masked man stumbling and splashing in the river as the river jet-boaters reached him.

Soon Joe and Frank were at the bluff where they had last seen Wendy. They took a moment to stop and look behind them. They listened carefully as their hearts pounded and they drew rapid breaths. Other than the burble of the water and the sounds of frogs and crickets, they heard nothing.

"We'd hear them if they were coming after us," Frank said to Joe. "I think we've lost them . . . for now."

Joe looked around. "Where's Wendy?" he asked his brother.

"Let's keep going. I'm sure we'll find her," Frank said, but Joe thought he noticed a little uncertainty in Frank's normally calm and confident voice.

They ran until they reached Niagara Junior. Joe stopped and looked at the crest of the rapids. The shredded raft and saw blades were gone.

"Our masked friend must have covered his tracks before he came after us," Frank said.

"If it's the same guy," Joe said. "What if there are a couple of them in the same disguise? I'll bet half the men in this county own hunter's camouflage suits."

"We'd better find Wendy," Frank said.

Soon Joe and Frank had passed all of the rapids they had rafted through only an hour before, with no sign of Wendy or the masked man.

Peering upriver, Frank spotted a dim light. As he and Joe drew closer, they saw two men seated on the bank of the river. A shiny aluminum canoe was beached onshore. The two men were both wearing green rubber hip waders. One of them stood in the middle of the river, fishing. The other sat on the bank, eating a sandwich. A fishing rod lay on the ground next to him. Nearby was a gas lantern on top of a cooler. Scattered on the bank were papers and empty cans.

Frank and Joe crouched on the cliff above the river to get a good look at the men. Suddenly, behind them, they heard a soft whirring sound. Joe turned his head and saw a tiny red light in the shadows.

"Don't move. Don't make a sound!" came Wendy's voice from the shadows. She was videotaping the two men.

Frank figured out that the two men were Mayor George Latimer and Carl Vissen. He told Joe, and they listened carefully to the men's voices, which carried over the water and echoed against the cliff.

"We're close, Carl, really close," the mayor said to the developer.

"How long have they been here?" Joe whispered to Wendy.

"About five minutes," Wendy hissed back. "Now shut up."

Vissen cast his fishing line downriver. "I don't know, George. We really have to make sure that tomorrow goes well."

Latimer wiped his lips with a paper towel, then tossed the towel into the water.

"Good one, George," Wendy said to herself as she zoomed in on the mayor.

"You should have given me a week to get the presentation finished," Vissen said, slapping a mosquito on his forearm.

"How could I?" Latimer asked. "You saw the free-for-all at that town meeting. Strike while the iron is hot, Carl, and the irons are as hot as they're going to get."

Vissen made his way back to shore as he reeled in. "My media people will just barely have the video finished by tomorrow. I've got them pulling all-nighters now."

Latimer said, "The longer we stall, the more ammunition we give the other side."

"I know, I know," said Vissen as he climbed up onto the bank.

Joe said softly to Wendy, "We've got to get back to camp."

"Shh!" Wendy said. "This is just getting good."

Frank whispered, "The sniper knows we're out here."

"About time to call it a night, wouldn't you say?" Vissen asked the mayor, who agreed.

"I think I'll just empty this cooler so it's not so heavy on our way back," Vissen said. He brought the cooler down to the shore and lifted the lid. Then he took out some wrappers and napkins and threw them in the river.

"Stay in the light, Vissen," Wendy murmured.

Vissen continued to talk to Latimer. "I'll deliver my part, George. You'd just better make sure those state funds find their way to my accounts when you promised they would."

"Check it out," Wendy whispered to Frank and Joe.

Joe watched the figure on the bank. Vissen took a bottle out of the cooler and poured the contents into the water. He then threw the bottle in too.

"I can't stomach this," Wendy said.

"Oh, no, not—" Joe didn't want to watch what happened next.

Vissen looked at the contents of the cooler, shrugged, and tipped the whole thing over, spilling cans, bags, ice, and garbage into the waters of the Big Bison.

"I hope all of that was recorded," Wendy said as she entered her father's camp. "There should have been enough light from their lantern. I wish I could have followed Vissen and Latimer down the river."

Frank and Joe were right behind her. "We couldn't stay out there," Frank said. "Who knows where that guy is now?"

Joe tapped Frank on the shoulder. "It seems we have a visitor."

Roger MacKendrick was waiting for them, sitting in the Adirondack chair on the porch of Owen's cabin.

"Evening, folks," Roger said. "Nice night to

be out rafting. Too bad it's against the law to be on the river after dark."

Wendy hid her camera bag behind her back. "I can explain everything."

Roger stood up. His right arm was still in the sling, and he flinched slightly with pain when he moved. He held a flashlight in his left hand. "I got a phone call saying three kids were nearly drowned out there on the rapids. It didn't take a rocket scientist to figure out who those three were. I suppose you can explain this."

The ranger switched on the flashlight and shone it on the ground. Lying there, looking like a maimed jellyfish, was what was left of the raft.

"I found this here when I drove up," Roger said. "Whoever called me must have found it. Now, you'd better tell me what's been going on out here tonight."

Wendy, Frank, and Joe recounted what happened on the river. No one referred to the fact that Wendy had taped certain incidents.

"I warned you guys," Roger said, "that it's not safe out here these days. Wendy, you'll probably lose your guide's license over this. You should know better, but you're every bit as pigheaded as your dad. There's no excuse for your pals."

Joe spoke up. "But you should know what's going on. We were trying to get some information about—"

"I *do* know what's going on," Roger interrupted. "That's part of my job. Trust me, I'm trying to get to the bottom of this whole mess. But I can't do it with you guys snooping around night and day."

Roger headed back toward his pickup truck, then stopped and spoke to Frank and Joe once more.

"Look, you guys, I'm grateful you took me to the hospital and that you want to find out who shot me and Wendy's dad. But Two Trees and I can handle it. Do us all a favor, just clear out of town. The sooner the better, you got me?"

The next morning Joe and Frank entered the lobby of Gehenna Memorial Hospital a few minutes before visiting hours were to begin. After they signed in, the receptionist behind the desk walked over to them.

"I'm afraid Mr. Watson has just come back from surgery."

"Surgery?" Joe asked. "Again?"

The receptionist nodded. "The doctor had to go back in to remove the bullet."

"Does that mean we can't see him?" Frank asked.

"Only immediate family." She glanced down the hall. "Here's his doctor. Maybe you can ask him about Mr. Watson."

The doctor who had tended Owen and Roger recognized Joe and Frank and approached them, wearing a serious expression.

"How is Mr. Watson?" Frank asked.

"I got the bullet out, but it was touch and go. You never know with a wound like Owen's. That bullet could've easily paralyzed him. But I think he'll be all right. Doreen and Wendy are with him in recovery."

"Can't we talk to him for just a minute?" Joe pleaded.

"Sorry," the doctor said. "I bent the rules once for you two. I can't do it again. Besides, Owen won't be able to put more than two words together. He's pretty sedated. Maybe tomorrow."

"Now what?" Joe asked his brother as the doctor disappeared down the corridor.

"Remember what Doreen told us yesterday?" Frank asked Joe. "She said, 'Ask Owen what he's got locked in his files.' Well, since we can't ask him, maybe we should go find out."

"I thought you didn't want to go digging around in Owen's office," Joe said.

Frank rubbed his chin with his hand. "That was a few gunshots ago. Besides, it's not like we're breaking and entering."

Joe smiled and pulled a large ring of keys from his pocket—Owen's keys.

Inside the cabin, the Hardys began to methodically sift through the files.

"Look at this one," Frank said as he took a folder from a drawer. "It looks like financial statements and reports."

Frank spread the papers across Owen's smooth

wooden desk. "It seems that state money for environmental protection and things like trails and campgrounds has gone other places."

Joe was sitting in front of another file cabinet. "How could that happen?" he asked.

Frank scanned the photocopied forms on the desk. "Seems like the state money was paid to the mayor's office, and Latimer used it for other things."

"What kinds of other things?"

Frank shuffled through some more papers. "It's kind of hard to trace. . . ."

Joe grinned. "I'm sure it is."

Frank grabbed one sheet. "Found it! Huge payments to some kind of land development company. It's called New Gehenna Partners. Vissen said something to Latimer last night about state funds."

"Check out what I found!" Joe said. "River jets were banned on the Big Bison until two years ago, when the laws were changed."

"I wonder who got them changed?" Frank mused.

Joe pulled several manila folders out of the file cabinet. "I'm sure we'll find out if we keep digging."

Frank looked up from his papers. "Owen might not appreciate us going through his files," he said. "We could get in a lot of trouble, so I think we should tell him."

Joe shrugged and said, "We're *already* in a lot

of trouble. What's a little more?" He pulled a legal document out of another file. "Here's something signed by Artis Haney, Lee Roy Samuels, and a lot of other guys with businesses in town. They say Owen Watson has an unfair hold on the use of the river."

"That *is* how Owen makes his money—guiding rafting tours," Frank said.

"Well, these people demand equal use of the Big Bison for all kinds of activities, not just rafting. They say Owen's environmental campaign is just a front for making money . . . that he really doesn't care about the environment at all."

Frank walked over and looked at the papers. "How can they say that?" he asked.

"Maybe we should look at Owen's bank accounts," Joe said.

Frank examined another sheet of paper. "Here's something about a virus in domestic sheep that's killing off all the wild bighorn sheep in the canyon."

Just then Frank and Joe heard a noise outside. They glanced at each other and both ran for the office door.

But before they got there, a side window shattered. A brown bottle with a flaming rag stuffed into the neck smashed on the floor.

"A Molotov cocktail!" Joe yelled.

Gasoline spread across the floor, and a second later the entire room burst into searing yellow flames.

Chapter

12

FRANK GRABBED THE CELLULAR TELEPHONE from Owen's desk and followed Joe toward the back of the flaming cabin.

Joe kicked open the back door of the cabin. Cool air rushed in. Taking big breaths of air, Frank and Joe ran out into the woods. Inside the cabin, flames spread up the walls, turning the simple cloth curtains on the windows into sheets of fire.

Frank quickly dialed 911 and reported the fire. In the distance Joe heard the sound of a boat engine.

"You Hardys are nothing but trouble," Billy Two Trees said.

Behind him the blackened timbers of Owen's

cabin smoked. The local volunteer firefighters hadn't arrived to put out the fire until long after all of the papers and supplies in the cabin were ashes.

"I was on my way out to see you two this morning anyway," Chief Two Trees said, out of earshot of the firefighters. "A couple of the locals said they were out on the river last night, doing some hunting."

"Bats," Joe said, glancing at Frank.

"I am not bats," Chief Two Trees said.

"No, I meant they were *shooting* at bats," Joe added.

The chief just glared at Joe, then continued. "Somebody took a potshot at them. Roger MacKendrick says you guys were out on the river last night."

"So were the gunrunners," Joe said quickly. He and Frank told Chief Two Trees what had happened to them out on the river.

"I'm beginning to think I *should* have locked you two up for grand theft auto," the chief mumbled. "It would have kept you out of trouble. And what were you doing in Owen's cabin?"

"Well . . . we found a lot of interesting stuff in his files," Joe said sheepishly.

"Oh, ho!" Chief Two Trees crowed. "You were going through Owen's *private* files, which are now conveniently in ashes. I'll have to add that one to your rap sheet. Right now I have a firebombing to investigate," the chief said sternly.

"You know, I will regret the day Frank and Joe Hardy came to this place as long as I live. Am I making myself clear?"

Frank and Joe both stared silently at the ground. Saying anything more would only dig them into a deeper hole.

The next afternoon in the Gehenna Diner, Claire, the waitress, delivered cheeseburgers and sodas to Joe, Frank, and Wendy.

Frank spoke as Joe attacked his burger. "I think half the people in this town would like us to pack up and go home right now."

"I wouldn't," Wendy said. "As a matter of fact, I need you to stick around, at least for the town meeting tonight."

"Is this about your video project?" Frank asked.

"All I need from you is some minor technical assistance," Wendy said eagerly.

"What kind of assistance?" Joe asked.

"Just put the tape in the VCR and push the Play button when I tell you to," Wendy said.

Frank sipped his soda, then said, "I don't know what you've got planned, but if you want, maybe we should go to the town hall and check it out now."

"That's a great idea," Wendy said. "I can see where all the video equipment is so there are no surprises tonight."

After finishing lunch, Wendy and the Hardys

paid Claire and headed for the Gehenna Town Hall.

They stood in the back of the hall, silently watching a crew of media specialists installing two huge projection television screens and an array of stereo speakers. Technicians were running cables and electrical cords all over the hall. Others were putting up extra lights on the speaker's platform.

In the back of the room was a huge control panel with dozens of levers and knobs to control the lighting, sound, and video images for Vissen's presentation.

Local news crews were setting up their equipment, too. Frank realized that Vissen was more than a local developer. The man definitely wanted to attract attention far and wide for his Gehenna Canyon development project. He wondered if Vissen had been the one who alerted the media to Owen's shooting and sent them to the hospital. Maybe Vissen would use any excuse to put the town on the map. Frank had realized while looking into Owen's files that the Save the Canyon Foundation needed newspapers and television for their cause, too.

"Whatever Carl Vissen plans to present at the town meeting tonight," Joe said, "he's leaving nothing to chance."

"You're right," Frank agreed. "This won't be any simple fireside chat with the locals."

"He may think he's got everything under control," Wendy said with a sly smile, "but believe me, he's in for a big surprise."

At eight o'clock that evening, the hall was packed with even more people than the previous meeting. Frank sat in a chair in the back corner, while Wendy and Joe hovered close to the control panel.

Mayor Latimer opened the special meeting with some remarks about the tensions and fighting in the area. Then he continued, "I'm sure if we all watch and listen to what Mr. Carl Vissen has prepared for us this evening, a lot of the questions we've been asking about the fate of our beloved canyon and river will be answered. So please, give your undivided attention to this program from Vissen Enterprises."

The audience quieted down as the lights in the hall dimmed. The two giant screens flickered, then the Vissen Enterprises corporate logo appeared, with a pompous fanfare. A deep, rumbling voice spoke about the importance of using natural resources responsibly while preserving the environment. This was accompanied by serene images of the canyon and the river.

At the control panel, several technicians frantically adjusted sound levels and shoved tapes in and out of tape decks. Frank thought that all of the chaos at the control panel was the result of all-night scrambling to assemble this presentation.

Wendy leaned over toward Joe and whispered in his ear, "I'm going out to pick up a little surprise." She handed him a videotape. "Count to ten, then stick this tape into one of the VCRs, hit Play, and stand back."

Wendy slipped out of the room. On the screen, the audience watched a montage of many successful Vissen resorts, followed by a computer-generated model of the resort Vissen planned to build in Gehenna Canyon.

A shot of Big Bison showed rafts, river jets, and canoes all calmly using the river, with no clashes or conflicts. Clever computer graphics, Frank thought to himself.

Joe stood close to the control panel. He counted to ten, then quickly jammed the tape into the empty VCR and hit the play button.

The video screens went black. Wendy's voice came over the sound system: "This is a message from the Save the Canyon Foundation. Take a look at how your mayor plans to protect the environment."

On the screen appeared a grainy image of Latimer throwing a paper towel into the river, which Wendy had videotaped the night before.

The audience howled with laughter at the shot of the mayor. The screen went black again, and Wendy's voice came back. "And this is what Carl Vissen plans to do to Big Bison River."

The screen showed Vissen dumping a bottle into the river, then the entire contents of the cooler. This time the audience whooped. Some people booed and hissed.

Vissen, who was seated in the front row, stood up and turned to the control panel. "Stop the tape!" he bellowed. "Turn up some lights!"

The technicians stopped the tape and the audio. Another technician brought up the lights on the speaker's platform. Vissen and Latimer rushed toward the microphone from opposite sides.

There were already two figures approaching the platform, ahead of Latimer and Vissen. Wendy pushed a wheelchair to the mike. Seated in the wheelchair was a very old Native American woman. She wore a wool sweater, baseball cap, and running shoes, along with a deerskin dress.

Wendy parked the wheelchair behind the microphone and adjusted the mike to the old woman's level. The local news crews dashed to the front of the room to capture the event.

The old woman spoke. "My ancestors lived in this canyon for hundreds of years . . . maybe even thousands."

Vissen shouted to the technicians, "Kill the mike!"

The woman continued, "This land is sacred to my people . . ." Suddenly the microphone went dead. But the woman had a battery-powered megaphone and continued to speak.

"Today everyone fights over how to use the canyon. I am here to say that the canyon cannot be *used*. If we want to continue to enjoy the waters, we must preserve the canyon as it is right now and make it a national park."

Billy Two Trees grabbed Joe's wrists from behind. Before Joe realized what happened, the chief of police had him in handcuffs. "Sorry, Joe," Chief Two Trees said. "I have to arrest you for disturbing the peace."

The chief dragged Joe through the audience and toward the speakers' platform. He yanked Joe onto the platform, then grabbed Wendy's wrists and cuffed them.

Chief Two Trees shouted out, "This meeting is over. I'm arresting you for disturbing the peace and causing a public nuisance, Wendy Watson." He turned to the old woman in the wheelchair, looked her in the eye, and said, "You too, Grandmother."

Chapter

13

"I DON'T SEE WHY you had to do that, Billy," the old woman said. She sat in her wheelchair, which was parked in the middle of a jail cell. "I was just speaking what I believe. Didn't I teach you that?"

Billy Two Trees put a key into the lock of the cell. "But, Grandmother, why did you agree to bust up a public meeting like that?"

"I'm exercising my right of freedom of speech," the chief's grandmother said. "Besides, this nice young girl asked me to speak."

Wendy sat on a bench in the cell, holding her head in her hands. At that she looked up and said, "That's right. I did ask Mrs. Two Trees to help us."

Joe was sitting next to Wendy. Frank stood

outside the cell. "All my brother did was play the tape," Frank said.

"You can't throw him in jail for that," Wendy said. "My mom's a lawyer. She'll get the charges dropped."

Mrs. Two Trees continued, "You should listen to what this young lady has to say, Billy. She's smart."

Chief Two Trees closed his eyes. "Grandmother, I've been listening to her for an hour now. I'd appreciate it if both you and Wendy here exercised your freedom of speech some other time. Now, if you'll all listen to me—"

Mrs. Two Trees frowned. "Why? You never come to see me anymore. I'm always saying I have to get myself arrested to get you to talk to me. Well, Billy, here I am."

Chief Two Trees opened the door of the cell. "Grandmother, Joe, I really can't hold you as accessories. Wendy made a full statement earlier, and she's taking full responsibility for your actions."

"I can leave?" Joe asked.

"Please," the chief said wearily. "Leave town. Leave Montana. Just leave me alone."

Mrs. Two Trees locked the brakes of her wheelchair. "I'm not going anywhere," she stated firmly. "I'm staying with this young lady."

Doreen Falk-Watson entered the jail just then. "Chief, can I talk to you?" she asked. Doreen spoke softly to him, so that no one else could hear, then walked over to the cell.

Wendy stood and said to her mother, "Are you here to bail me out?"

"No, Wendy," Doreen said. "I'm afraid I'm not. I've decided to let you spend the night in jail."

Wendy's jaw dropped. "But why, Mom?"

Doreen pursed her lips, then spoke in a tense, measured voice. "I've seen what's been happening to you. Every day you become more and more like your father."

"So?" Wendy said defiantly.

"I've been working very hard for the Ranchers' Guild, trying to help all of the factions in our town get along. In one night you might have ruined years of my work."

"I'll bail her out," came a voice from the doorway.

"Now what?" Chief Two Trees said.

The head of the Ranchers' Guild, Nick Krakowski, stood in the doorway. "Just tell me what her bail is, Billy," Nick said. "It's worth it to catch Vissen trashing the river."

Doreen was shocked. "Nick!" she said. "You can't! Carl Vissen and I are supposed to meet—"

Nick interrupted Doreen, grinning. "I've been waiting for somebody to take that clown down a peg. I've never been able to stand him . . . always strutting around thinking he can buy this town. Wendy, my fearless young radical, it was worth every penny."

Nick paid Wendy's bail, and Wendy and Doreen left the jail with him. Mrs. Two Trees still refused to move. "Billy, lock the cell," she said. "Then sit down here and talk to me."

As Joe and Frank left the jail, they heard the chief say wearily, "Whatever you say, Grandmother."

The next morning Joe and Frank sat with Wendy at her father's bedside in the hospital. Frank related what they had seen in Owen's files. Then Wendy told her father about the town meeting and her arrest.

"Aren't you proud of me, Dad?" she asked Owen.

Even though Owen was still sedated, he could still work up a reasonable anger. "Did you stop and think what could have happened to you or Joe or that old woman?" he barked. "There are people out there who tried to kill me and *did* burn out my cabin."

"But, Dad, I thought you would have done the same thing," Wendy pleaded.

"Yes, *I* would have," Owen said. "The whole town expects it from me. I'm everyone's favorite enviro-freak, not you. Let's keep it that way."

Frank sat up, remembering the plastic action figures at the scene of two crimes and the words scrawled on the cabin door. "Who calls you an 'enviro-freak'?" Frank asked Owen.

"That crazy militia group—the Knights of Liberty," Owen said. "They like to think they can overthrow the government. I've always thought of them as a bunch of overgrown boys playing soldier."

"Soldiers need guns," Frank said. "Do you think they're the ones who are running guns on the river?"

"Who else?" Owen said, then turned to Wendy. "Let Billy Two Trees and Roger Mac-Kendrick handle this, Wendy."

"What about Vissen?" Wendy asked. "Don't we have to stop him?"

"Wendy, we have to stop *everybody*," Owen said. "Not just Vissen, but the ranchers, the boaters, the loggers, the forest service . . ."

"Loggers?" Frank asked. "We didn't know about any loggers."

Owen answered, "Doreen and I put a stop to logging years ago. But the ban was temporary. The logging and mining rights will be up for grabs soon, along with a lot of other rights. I'm telling you, a national park—"

Wendy rolled her eyes. "Dad, you're a broken record. *And* you're supposed to rest."

Owen had one more piece of advice. "If you want to get the goods on Carl Vissen, do it legally. See what you can find out about New Gehenna Partners."

A nurse entered Owen's room, announced the end of visiting hours, and ordered Wendy, Frank, and Joe to leave.

In the hospital parking lot, Wendy seemed upset. "I've never been so afraid," she said. "Now everybody will be furious with me—the mayor, Vissen, those militia men who shot Dad . . ."

"Why do you think they're the ones who did it?" Joe asked.

"It makes sense," Wendy said. "I'm sure they wanted Dad off the river. Sooner or later he would have found out about the gunrunning."

"Right," Frank said. "What happens if the canyon actually becomes a national park?"

"For one thing, there'd be a lot more supervision than one lone state forest ranger," Wendy said. "They couldn't run weapons up and down the river."

"But they'd find another way to get the weapons moved around," Joe interjected. "Right now the river is the easiest route to use and the hardest to trace . . . as long as there are no floaters."

"Wendy, how far did your father get on his national park campaign?" Frank asked.

"Pretty far," Wendy replied. "Our representative in Congress was going to introduce a bill in the next session to start the wheels turning."

Frank narrowed his eyes. "Who knew about that?"

Wendy thought for a moment. "I did, and I think Mom helped Dad make some of those connections and did a lot of the legal paperwork."

Frank wondered silently if Wendy's mother had anything to reveal. And he knew there was only one way to find out.

When Frank and Joe entered the office of the Ranchers' Guild, they found Doreen at her desk, using the computer. Nick's office was empty.

"What brings you guys back?" Doreen asked.

"We need some answers to some pretty difficult questions," Joe said.

Frank attempted to smooth over his brother's brashness. "Do you have a minute to talk to us?"

Doreen's spine stiffened, but she maintained a professional and pleasant attitude. "I have a couple of minutes. Just remember that as a lawyer I must protect my clients."

Joe began. "Why don't you want your daughter to turn out like Owen? Are you opposed to Owen's campaign?"

A look of concern passed over Doreen's face before she replied. "No. I still like to support Owen's causes. Even though I couldn't stay married to the man, I do think he's right. So does Nick."

"So Owen and your boss aren't enemies?" Frank asked.

"Nick and Owen could get along if they just tried," Doreen said. "Owen goes too far and thinks the ranchers should get out of the canyon altogether. That's just not possible. Even a national park could still extend land use to the ranchers. That's why I never saw working for the

121

ranchers as a conflict of interest. If Owen has an enemy, it's not Nick."

"Who do you think shot those sheep?" Joe asked. "The Knights of Liberty?"

"Those loonies," Doreen said. "Every now and then one of their people shows up on the TV news, always wearing some silly ski mask and hunting clothes, ranting against 'invaders' in the canyon. I always took that to mean Owen's floaters. But I suppose you could take that to mean our ranchers as well."

Frank took another tack. "Owen told us that you and he stopped the logging in the canyon. Could some logger hold a grudge against Owen?"

Doreen laughed. "Owen stopped the logging out of guilt."

"What do you mean?" Joe asked.

Doreen paused a moment, as if hesitating to tell the story, then spoke. "When I first met Owen years ago, he *was* a logger. In fact, he and Roger MacKendrick started out side by side cutting timber. Owen realized that the logging was destroying the natural wilderness and started shooting his mouth off about it. That got Owen fired, and MacKendrick got a promotion."

"How?" Frank asked.

Doreen sighed. "Roger MacKendrick told the president of the corporation that Owen was a troublemaker."

Frank pursued this train of thought. "How did MacKendrick end up in the forest service?"

Doreen took a deep breath. "Well, Owen and I managed to get the loggers out before the old-growth forest was touched. It was a major legal victory, but MacKendrick lost his job. I don't think Roger ever forgave Owen. Roger then got into the forest service through some business connection."

"And who was that?" Joe asked.

Doreen looked at the clock, then looked down at the calendar on her desk. "I'm sorry," she said in a cold and impersonal tone. "I have an appointment downtown. I'll have to ask you to leave now."

The Hardys complied. It was midafternoon, and they decided to go to the diner. They weren't really hungry, but they weren't sure where else to go. They sat in a back booth, near the pay telephone.

"Wendy's mother isn't telling us everything she knows," Joe said to Frank.

Frank nodded in agreement. "She told us she was protecting herself and her clients. But I think she's given us something to go on. Remember, Owen told us to find out what we could about New Gehenna Partners."

"How can we do that?" Joe sighed. "It's not like we have a lot of information at our fingertips."

Frank's expression brightened. "You've done it again, baby brother!" he exclaimed. Joe hated it when Frank called him that. Frank knew Joe hated it.

"What have I done this time?" Joe asked.

Frank didn't answer. He stood up and said, "Ask Claire if we can tie up the telephone line for a little while."

Frank rushed out the front door of the diner. Joe went over to the counter, where Claire sat reading a newspaper. "Mind if we use the pay phone, Claire?" he inquired.

"Going to call your girlfriend, honey? That pretty little Watson girl?"

Joe said, a little defensively, "She's *not* my girlfriend." Joe thought of Vanessa Bender back in Bayport. Right now he wanted to call her.

"Sure you can use the phone," she drawled. "It's not like there's a line of folks waiting to use it."

"Thanks, Claire," Joe said, returning to the booth.

Frank burst back in with the notebook computer from the van and an external modem. He handed the modem to Joe, telling him, "Hook us up to the pay phone, Joe. We're going surfing."

Joe hooked up the phone to the modem as Frank started up the computer. Within a matter of minutes Frank and Joe were on the Internet.

"That's the first time I've ever seen anybody doing that in this diner," Claire observed as she watched curiously over Frank's shoulder.

Joe and Frank were both seated on the same side of the table, watching the screens fly by as they searched one database after another.

"There ought to be some record of New Gehenna Partners," Frank mumbled. "Deeds or legal filings."

Joe made a suggestion. "Try tracking down a profile of Carl Vissen. He's a public figure."

Frank's nimble fingers dashed over the keyboard. A moment later Vissen's face flashed up on the screen, followed by a lengthy profile. Frank and Joe both scanned it quickly.

"Check this out," Joe said softly. "Carl Vissen owns a couple of logging companies."

"Yup. And mining companies, too," Frank added.

Frank tapped into the annual report of Vissen Enterprises. "It looks as if resorts aren't Carl Vissen's main business," he said to Joe. "He's into strip mining, lumber, paper . . ."

"A heavy-duty polluter," Joe said.

"Bingo!" Frank exclaimed.

"What did you find?" Joe asked.

"The prospectus for New Gehenna Partners . . . a Vissen company," Frank said.

Joe glanced over at the counter. Claire had gone back to her newspaper. Frank logged out and told Joe to disconnect the modem.

"This is what they didn't want us to know," Frank gasped. "Vissen plans to cash in on the mining and logging rights in the Gehenna Canyon . . . that's where the real money is as far as Vissen is concerned. The resort is a cover."

"What do you say we drop in on Carl Vissen?" Joe asked. Frank and Joe headed for their van.

* * *

An assistant wearing a navy suit and a brush cut announced Frank and Joe Hardy's arrival at Vissen Enterprises. On the intercom Vissen said tersely, "Show them right in."

After leading them to Vissen's office the assistant indicated chairs for the Hardys to sit in, in front of Vissen's desk.

Rather than being his usual warm, charming self, Vissen seemed tense and edgy. "I didn't appreciate what you and that Watson girl pulled the other night," he said angrily. "I suppose you've come to apologize for invading my privacy."

Joe was about to speak when the door to Vissen's office flew open. Vissen's assistant shouted, "I couldn't stop him, Mr. Vissen."

Vissen's jaw dropped, and his face turned ashen. Frank and Joe whirled around.

In the doorway stood the masked sniper, his hand in his pocket. Joe could see the outline of a pistol in the man's camouflage jacket pocket. Joe's eyes darted around the room as he looked for something he could use as a weapon or a shield. He saw a chair on wheels and was about to go for it when he heard the distinct sound of a hammer cocking.

"Don't even think of moving one inch," the masked man threatened.

Chapter
14

"I'LL GIVE YOU TILL MIDNIGHT to get out of town," the gunman growled to Joe and Frank. "If you're not gone, you'll be *gone,* got me? You, too, Vissen. If you think you can buy the canyon, I'll see to it you buy the farm."

The masked man turned around sharply and shoved Vissen's assistant against the chairs where Joe and Frank sat. They rose to their feet and caught him.

Vissen yelled into the phone, "Get security over to my office! There's a lunatic with a gun in here!"

Frank and Joe raced out the front door of Vissen Enterprises and looked around. There was no sign of the sniper anywhere. They split up and ran in opposite directions through the modern office complex, and scanned all of the roads in every direction, but the sniper seemed to have vanished without a trace.

Frank and Joe ran back into Vissen's office. "You'd better call Billy Two Trees," Joe said.

Back in their cabin in Watson's camp a little later, Frank paced back and forth as Joe stretched out on the upper bunk bed.

"It *has* to be Artis Haney," Frank said conclusively. "He could be the head of the gunrunners. That four-by-four at the old hunters' camp with all the weapons in it came from Haney's dealership."

Joe sat up. "Wake up, Sherlock," he said. "The guy in the mask was talking to Artis Haney that night. I think it's Gordo Haney going psycho because I've been hanging out with Wendy."

Frank sat in an old wooden chair. "Doreen said that the Knights of Liberty showed up on the local news in ski masks and camouflage suits."

"So that's a kind of uniform," Joe said, "which any one of them could be wearing."

"Maybe we shouldn't be looking for one man," Frank said. "After all, there were two guys dressed the same way last night on the river."

Joe jumped down from the bunk. "Okay, Frank, say that Artis Haney was the one who shot Owen. Then suppose Artis set the booby trap for us on the river. It makes sense, if Artis and his son are involved in the gunrunning. But then who was Artis talking to at the hunters' camp?"

Frank sprung to his feet. "I have an idea. Maybe we should get back on the Net. Let's go to the diner. I'll drive."

Joe and Frank hooked their modem up to the pay phone in the diner before they sat down to order.

"You two back with that computer thing again?" Claire asked.

"Just for a minute," Joe said. "Two colas, please," he added.

"You got it," Claire said as she sauntered back toward the counter. "Maybe we should forget being a diner and become a truck stop on the information superhighway. What do you think, guys?"

Joe watched Frank dig into the Internet. He looked up at Claire and nodded. "Good idea, Claire."

Frank spoke softly to Joe. "A lot of these paramilitary groups use the Net to communicate. I think I'm getting close."

"There!" Joe pointed at the screen. "Go to that page."

The screen flashed with a logo for the Knights of Liberty. "They're inviting their friends to call them for supplies," Joe said, scanning the text on the screen.

" 'Supplies' could mean guns and ammo,"

Frank said. "Here's an E-mail address . . . and here's a phone number."

"I recognize that number!" Joe exclaimed. He reached into his pocket and fished out his wallet, then removed the scrap of paper he had taken earlier from the bulletin board at the diner. Joe held the paper up against the screen.

"There's our man," Joe said. "Lee Roy Samuels."

"Please, just listen to us," Frank said to Billy Two Trees.

"This better be good," Chief Two Trees said. He didn't invite the Hardys to sit down, though there were two chairs in his office.

"Look, we can take you to the cave where we saw the weapons in crates," Frank stated emphatically. "You already confiscated the weapons in that four-by-four that was rented from Haney's dealership."

Chief Two Trees interrupted Frank. "There are some legal complications. You see, Haney's not responsible for the way his rentals are used. And it takes time to check out those unlicensed weapons. The agents from the ATF aren't coming till next week. There's no way of knowing who rented that truck, anyway."

"Didn't Haney have a rental contract?" Joe asked.

"Cash," the chief said. "Only a receipt for cash. Haney seemed as surprised as you were about the guns. Look, fellows, I can't just move in on any of these men without something a little more concrete. If I could only catch someone making a deal over those weapons, then I could arrest them on the spot."

"Suppose we could arrange that," Joe said. "Would you do it?"

Chief Two Trees scowled. "Don't you two cowboys think you can just charge in like the cavalry in some old Western and save the day. You take the law into your own hands, and you're no better than those militia kooks."

"Wait," Joe said. "We have a plan."

"We'll have to maneuver carefully," Frank said. "They already want us out of the way."

"They're not the only ones," the chief quipped.

"But we might be able to trip them up for you," Joe said.

Chief Two Trees took a deep breath. "I can't believe I'm asking this, but what do you two have up your sleeves?"

Joe and Frank told him the scheme they had cooked up. When they had finished, the chief leaned back in his chair and looked up at the ceiling. "It just might work," he said with a sigh.

"So are you with us?" Joe asked eagerly.

"I said it *might* work," Chief Two Trees said.

Just then Roger MacKendrick came in. "What are you two up to now?" MacKendrick asked, spotting Frank and Joe.

"Roger, our friends here have come up with a

scheme that could stop all the fighting on the Big Bison," Chief Two Trees said. He went on to outline what the boys had told him.

"It's risky," MacKendrick said after he'd listened to the plan. "What do you think, Billy?"

Two Trees looked intensely into Joe's eyes, then Frank's. "I may regret this . . . but let's give it a shot."

Nick Krakowski looked across the office at Doreen, then at Joe, Frank, and Wendy. He took a deep breath. "What do you think, Doreen?"

"I've been trying to get all of these groups together for weeks now. I think it could work," Doreen said.

"Great!" Frank said. "Nick, the first step is to call Artis Haney."

"Right away," Nick said as he picked up the telephone and dialed. He waited a second, then spoke. "Haney, this is Nick Krakowski. I'm sitting here with Wendy Watson. Will you talk with her?"

There was a brief pause, then Nick said, "Wendy, pick up the other line."

Wendy picked up an extension. Frank, Joe, and Doreen all sat quietly, almost afraid to breathe.

"Hi, Mr. Haney," Wendy said. "I think you should know that I'm officially speaking for my dad and the Save the Canyon Foundation."

Nick Krakowski added, "And I'm speaking on the record for the Ranchers' Guild. I think the time has come for us all to bury the hatchet and get on the same side. I don't think any of us wants to keep fighting."

"If we don't all work together from now on, we're *all* going to lose the Gehenna Canyon to Vissen," Wendy said. "He's got plans not only for a resort, but also for logging and mining in the canyon. I don't think you and your group want that any more than we do."

There was a pause. Nick scowled and said, "Look, Artis, we all know about the Knights of Liberty, and we all know you're a member, so don't pretend you're not. If we can present a united front against Vissen, we can keep our land and our river. Once his plan goes down the tubes, we can all start fighting again, if you'd like."

Nick covered the mouthpiece of the telephone with his hand and said softly to Frank and Joe, "He's laughing."

Wendy got back on the phone. "Mr. Haney, is there a place we can all meet and talk tonight?" Another pause. "What time?" Wendy glanced at Frank. Frank held up six fingers.

Nick said, "How is six o'clock, Haney? Fine? Then let's meet out at your dealership, okay? We'll see you in an hour."

As Wendy and Nick hung up the phones, Doreen gave a thumbs-up sign to Joe and Frank.

"So far, so good," Joe said. "Now we have to talk to Samuels."

* * *

133

Lee Roy Samuels changed the TV channel with his remote as Joe and Frank opened the door of his office. "Been on the TV lately, boys?" Samuels sneered. "Or is your fifteen minutes of fame over?"

"Mr. Samuels, we came to apologize," Joe said. "We're sorry we accused you of trying to shoot Owen Watson."

"Yes," Frank said. "Now we know who really did it, and we know it wasn't you."

"Oh, really?" Samuels said, becoming interested. "Who did it?"

"As it turns out, we saw the sniper on videotape," Frank said, trying to seem casual. "It's Artis Haney."

"That's crazy!" Samuels shouted. "Haney can't even shoot straight. Besides, I know where Haney was when Watson was shot."

"How do you know?" Joe asked as offhandedly as he could.

"Why, he was on his cellular phone talking to me," Samuels declared. "I heard the shot in the background."

Frank remained calm. "Why was he calling you from the river?"

"We have similar . . . *business* interests," Samuels said. "We often talk on our cell phones."

"Did it have something to do with that little operation and the 'supplies' you're offering on your Internet page?" Joe asked. He watched for the man's reaction very carefully.

Samuels started to sweat. "I'm afraid I don't have the slightest idea what you boys are talking about," he said.

"That's too bad," Joe said. "Because Billy Two Trees mentioned that he knew all about what the Knights of Liberty have been doing on the river."

Samuels grinned. "Now, boys, I know most of the men in that group. They're my best customers. Law-abiding citizens, all of them. Sportsmen."

"That may be true," Frank said. "Still, we heard Billy say he and the Feds were going to bust it all up at the old hunters' camp later tonight." Frank and Joe rose to leave.

"Mr. Samuels, we just wanted to say we're sorry, and we're willing to testify that you're not the sniper," Joe said sincerely. "That's all."

"Thanks, partners," Samuels drawled. "Thanks a heap."

Frank and Joe left the office and walked past their own black van, through a small stand of trees, and joined Billy Two Trees. Chief Two Trees watched Samuels's office through a pair of binoculars.

Samuels emerged about two minutes later. He locked the door behind him, then got in his car.

"I'll bet you ten bucks he's going straight to Haney," Frank said to Billy.

"I'm not a gambling man," the chief replied. "But I'll bet ten bucks you're right." The chief jumped in his truck. "I'll follow him," he said.

135

"We'll be right behind you," Joe replied. Chief Two Trees followed Samuels at a safe distance. Frank and Joe got into their van to follow the chief. "Let's go!" Joe said as Frank started the engine and put the van in gear.

"You're not going anywhere," came a voice from the back of the van. Gordo Haney reached around the passenger seat and wrapped his left arm around Joe's throat. Joe reached up and grabbed Gordo's arm with both hands and tried to pull it away from his throat.

Then Joe heard a swift clicking noise.

In his right hand Gordo held a switchblade.

Chapter

15

FRANK SLAMMED ON THE BRAKES. Joe jerked forward but was stopped by his shoulder belt. Caught off balance, Gordo Haney slammed into the back of Joe's seat. His knife clattered to the floor.

Frank reached over and grabbed Gordo's left wrist with his right hand. He twisted it upward, releasing Joe's neck, then yanked it forward, pinning Gordo between the front seats.

"Let go of me!" Gordo wailed.

Joe quickly grabbed Gordo's right arm and said, "Not until you tell us what you're doing in our van."

Joe opened the side door and wrestled Gordo Haney out of the van. Gordo struggled but was no match for Joe. In a split second, Joe slammed Gordo against the side of the black van.

Frank reached down and snatched the knife from the floorboard, then jumped out of the driver's seat. He ran around to the other side, where Joe had Gordo's face pressed up against the van. "You'd better do some talking," Frank said to Gordo.

"Let me go," Gordo said. "I promise I won't try anything."

"You'd better not," Joe said. He slowly released Gordo.

Haney sat down on the shoulder at the side of the road, rubbing his wrists. "I didn't shoot Wendy's dad, and neither did my old man," he muttered.

"We know you didn't," Frank said. "But can you tell us who did?"

"I swear, I don't know," Gordo said. "I always kind of liked Mr. Watson. My dad never wanted me to go out with Wendy because of Watson. I never thought Owen's place would get, like, torched."

"Who did the firebombing?" Joe said sternly.

"Was it the Knights of Liberty?" Frank asked.

"No, man, no way," Gordo protested. "We just wanted to get you guys off the river."

"So we wouldn't find out about the guns, right?" Frank said.

"Yeah," Gordo said. "But you found out anyway. I never wanted to put those voodoo doll soldiers on your door, either. Dad made me."

"What about rigging our van to ignite?" Joe demanded.

"Yeah, I did that. Listen, you don't know what the Knights can make you do. They really mess with your head. They told me if I didn't get rid of you guys, they'd make me pay for it—in a *big* way. It was fun at first, but now, man, I'm really getting spooked."

This poor guy's in over his head, Frank thought.

Frank helped Joe get Gordo into the van. "All of this violence has to stop," Frank said. "You could really help us if you wanted to."

"I want it to stop, man," Gordo said as he huddled in the back of the van. "I really want it all to stop."

Frank pulled the van into the far end of Artis Haney's car lot. Joe and Frank had explained to Gordo their plan to draw Samuels to the car lot. After telling them about a back entrance to the office, Gordo led the Hardys through the body shop.

Gordo stopped dead in his tracks when he saw Billy Two Trees standing in the shop, outside the showroom office door, his pistol raised. Gordo looked nervous. Joe and Frank each put a hand on his shoulder.

"You can help us stop it, Gordo," Joe said.

"Be strong." The three of them walked through the door.

Wendy, her mother, and Nick Krakowski were seated around Haney's desk. Artis Haney's eyes widened when he saw Gordo with the Hardys, but he continued speaking to the others as if nothing was wrong.

"Of course, there are some things we'll never agree on," Haney said to Wendy. "But if you can guarantee that we'll get to keep running our boats on the Big Bison, then I think we can work something out."

Outside, Lee Roy Samuels pulled his car up to the front door. Artis Haney's muscles all tensed as he heard Samuels running up to the door.

"Haney!" Samuels yelled as he flung open the office door. "We got to get the guns out of the camp! Tonight!"

Samuels stopped dead when he saw Wendy, Doreen, Nick, Gordo, Frank, and Joe all staring at him.

Billy Two Trees burst through the back door. "Don't move, Samuels!" the police chief shouted, leveling his pistol at the boat dealer. Lee Roy Samuels turned and started to run toward his car.

Joe Hardy took off like a bolt of lightning and chased Samuels. He tackled him about ten feet from the car. Frank and Chief Two Trees were right behind him. The chief had Samuels in handcuffs in seconds.

Inside the office, Artis Haney tried to get

through the back door, but his son blocked the doorway.

"Give up, Dad," Gordo Haney said. "It's all over."

Artis turned and moved toward the front door, but was blocked by Billy Two Trees' massive frame.

"I think you'd better come along with me, Artis," the police chief said.

An hour later at the police station, Billy Two Trees was almost finished grilling Lee Roy Samuels. Because Joe and Frank had helped him catch Samuels, the chief let them sit in on the interrogation.

Samuels confessed that he and the Haneys, along with other members of the Knights of Liberty militia group, had been using the river to run weapons. He described a network of river jets, small camps, and 4 × 4 trucks used to spirit the weapons into the homes of the members without being caught—until the Hardys' trap snared them.

"What about Owen Watson?" Chief Two Trees asked. "Why did you shoot him?"

Samuels laughed, but it was a laugh without any joy in it. "You think we needed to shoot that enviro-freak? Owen Watson was no threat to us. We knew exactly when he came and went on the river."

"How about Ranger MacKendrick?" Joe asked. "Did you shoot him?"

"MacKendrick was shot?" Samuels said, appearing surprised by the news.

"The day before yesterday," Joe said. "My brother and I found him."

"How about shooting those sheep that were grazing up on the bluffs?" Chief Two Trees inquired.

Samuels looked disgusted. "What do you take us for, Two Trees?"

"Maybe you should tell me what you planned to do with all those guns and all that ammunition," Billy Two Trees said sternly.

Samuels looked away for a moment. "Let's say we're just looking to protect ourselves and our families from the United States government."

Billy Two Trees locked Samuels in the cell where he had detained Wendy, Joe, and his own grandmother shortly before. Artis Haney sat in the next cell.

"I'll talk to you tomorrow, Haney," Chief Two Trees said, then turned back to Joe and Frank. "You guys want to come back in the morning?" he asked.

"Sure," Joe said. "There are a lot of things that still don't add up."

"Well, don't worry about those things tonight," Chief Two Trees said. "Get some sleep."

The sun had set, and the few streetlights along Gehenna's main street had come on, casting a warm yellow glow in the humid summer air. Joe and Frank walked into the diner.

"I swear, I can't keep you two out of here," Claire said as Joe and Frank settled down into the corner booth. She winked at Frank. "The usual? Cheeseburger deluxe for you both?"

Frank nodded, and Claire walked the order back to the kitchen. Frank looked over at Joe. "Okay, so let's take all the gunrunning out of the picture," Frank said. "That still doesn't explain the rest. Who would want to shoot MacKendrick and threaten Vissen and us if it isn't the Knights? Not Krakowski, even though he hates Vissen."

"Okay, then, who did shoot MacKendrick?" Joe asked.

Claire brought Joe and Frank their burgers. "You talking about my little Roger?" she asked.

"Your Roger?" Joe responded.

Claire plunked a bottle of ketchup on the table. "Poor baby. It breaks my heart to see him with his arm in that sling." She headed back to the counter.

Joe grinned at Frank. "You mean MacKendrick is Claire's boyfriend?" Both Frank and Joe tried not to laugh. "He probably shot himself in the arm to get sympathy from Claire," Joe said.

Frank's expression suddenly turned serious. "Joe, you've done it one more time," Frank said.

"What have I done?" Joe asked, dunking a french fry in a pool of ketchup.

Frank waved his cheeseburger. "Think back to

when we found MacKendrick. He was shot in the right arm."

"Right," Joe said.

"He said he'd been shot a half hour before, but there wasn't enough blood," Frank said, getting the peculiar excitement Joe recognized when his older brother was close to solving a case. "That was a fresh wound. He was only grazed in the arm. Why didn't he drive himself to the hospital?"

"That's a good question," Joe said. "Why not?"

"Simple," Frank stated. "Because he wanted us to find him there. Remember, the doctor said it was more like a burn."

"Powder burns," Joe said.

Frank waved Claire over to the table. "Claire, would you please wrap up these burgers to go?"

"But—" Joe gasped with a mouthful of cheeseburger, looking longingly at his plate.

"Sure thing," Claire said, taking both plates away.

"What gives?" Joe asked.

Frank whispered, "We're going out to the ranger's station."

There were no vehicles parked at the ranger's station. A single light over the garage flooded the driveway but cast the concrete-block building into shadow. The full moon was just starting to rise.

Frank and Joe parked their black van down the highway where it couldn't be seen from the road. Silently they crept around the low building, looking carefully in all of the windows.

"Empty," Joe said.

The front door was closed, but—as Joe quickly found out—not locked. "I'm going in," he told Frank, who followed him.

Joe switched on the lights and circled the room a few times. "I don't know exactly what we're looking for but—" Joe sat down at the ranger's desk and looked at the wall behind him. "Frank! Up there!"

Frank looked up where the concrete-block wall met the acoustic tile ceiling. Deep in the ceiling tile was a bullet hole.

Frank ran outside and peered through the hole in the glass. "The bullet that broke the window hit the ceiling," Frank said to Joe, who was on the other side of the window.

Frank held his hand up to the bullet hole as if he held a pistol. "I couldn't hit your arm from here no matter how I tried," Frank told Joe. "Whoever fired this shot was standing on the ground, purposely aiming up at the ceiling."

Back into the empty office, Frank said, "The window was shot at close range. A bullet fired from a distance would have made a smaller hole."

Joe stood up. "Why would MacKendrick shoot

himself? And how could he have known we were going to the ranger's station that day?"

Frank paced around the small office. "Where were we right before that?"

Joe slid open the front drawer of MacKendrick's desk, then closed it. "Eating lunch at the diner," he said to Frank.

Frank began to pace more rapidly. "The waitress—Claire—heard everything we said. She must have called MacKendrick and told him we were coming. He must have hurried outside the building and fired a shot through the window. Then he shot himself. In the right arm, using his left hand. That explains the powder burns. Remember he told the doctor at the hospital he was left-handed."

Joe perched on the edge of MacKendrick's desk. "Suppose he didn't take the painkillers the doctor gave him. Maybe just aspirin."

"So he could get right back to the river to follow us."

"And he followed us to Niagara Junior, where he planted the saw blades," Joe said.

Frank picked up on Joe's thoughts. "Which is why he had the ripped-up raft. All of that fits. But why would MacKendrick do all this?"

Joe smiled. "For the same reason MacKendrick threatened Carl Vissen in our presence. To throw us off track. Make us think that MacKendrick and Vissen were victims of the Knights of Liberty."

"Quiet!" Frank said. Both Joe and Frank froze. They heard branches snapping on the ground outside the window. Frank switched out the desk lamp, then turned off the overhead fluorescent lights.

In the darkness outside the window, Frank and Joe saw the outline of a man, then heard the cocking of a shotgun.

"Get down!" Frank shouted. "He's got a gun!"

A shotgun blast exploded the window.

Chapter

16

JOE AND FRANK dropped behind the desk as the shotgun went off, showering the office with shards of glass.

The gunman used the barrel of his shotgun to clear the remaining glass from the window frame.

"I warned you two to leave town by midnight. You didn't listen. Too bad," the gunman said as he reloaded his shotgun and pointed it at Frank. Frank recognized MacKendrick's voice and could see the ranger's icy blue eyes through the ski mask he wore.

"Both of you, stand up where I can see you," MacKendrick said, leaning into the empty window frame. "Put your hands up!"

Joe stood from behind the desk. Both he and Frank put their hands in the air.

"You can't get away with this, MacKendrick," Frank said. "If you kill us—"

"Then nobody will be the wiser," the ranger said.

"Billy Two Trees will come looking for us," Joe said.

"He'll never find you," MacKendrick replied.

Frank moved very slowly away from the desk and toward the door. Joe inched toward the opposite wall. Quickly Frank realized that they had to keep MacKendrick talking.

"Why did you shoot Owen Watson?" Frank demanded. "Was it because he shut down the logging operation?"

"That's one reason," MacKendrick said, maintaining his position outside the window. "I've wanted to get back at Owen Watson for years. It wasn't until my boss told me to get him out of the way that I had the guts to try it."

Joe and Frank continued to inch imperceptibly in opposite directions.

"Who's your boss?" Frank asked.

"Carl, of course."

"Carl?" Joe asked. "Carl Vissen?"

"You would have found that out in Watson's files, but I made things a little too hot for you." MacKendrick laughed.

"Since we'll never know what was in there, why don't you tell us?" Joe asked the ranger.

"Why don't I just shoot you now and save my breath?"

Joe saw MacKendrick draw a bead on him. Suddenly Joe dove into the corner of the office.

"Hey!" MacKendrick yelled as he squeezed the trigger. Because MacKendrick tried to follow Joe's moving body, the shot hit the back wall of the office, shattering a glass-framed map of Gehenna Canyon.

"MacKendrick!" Frank shouted.

Roger MacKendrick swung the shotgun toward Frank. Just as he did, Frank switched on the desk lamp, blinding him. Then Frank thrust the lamp at MacKendrick's face.

The sudden glare of the bulb made MacKendrick flinch. He reached to cover his eyes and dropped his shotgun.

Joe, crouched beneath the window, sprang to his feet and grabbed MacKendrick's neck. Joe flipped the ranger through the empty window frame and onto the floor.

MacKendrick groaned with pain as his right shoulder hit the ground. "My shoulder!" MacKendrick howled.

"The same one you hurt when I threw you off the riverbank," Joe said.

MacKendrick tried to push himself up, but Joe pinned him to the floor. The ranger was in great pain, but it didn't affect the strength in his left arm. He reached up and shoved Joe away, then tried to pull himself to his feet.

Quickly Joe pushed over the heavy steel desk to where MacKendrick lay. Papers, pencils, and folders scattered on the floor with the shards of broken glass. Joe then tipped the desk over, pinning MacKendrick underneath. To be on the safe side, Joe put a chair on top of it. As he did, he noticed that Wendy's videotape had fallen out of one of the desk drawers.

When Joe noticed that MacKendrick still had the strength to heave the desk and chair off himself, he did what he had to do.

"Hand me the phone, Frank," Joe said. Frank did so, and then Joe settled himself in—in the chair on top of the desk. Finally MacKendrick gave up.

"Now that I've made myself comfortable," Joe said, "I think I'll give Chief Two Trees a call."

Within minutes the chief of the Gehenna police had Roger MacKendrick in handcuffs.

"This is the best workout these cuffs have had in ten years," Chief Two Trees quipped. "I wasn't sure they still worked."

"Nice outfit," Joe said, looking at MacKendrick's head-to-toe camouflage and ski mask. "But not exactly original."

"You should tell your girlfriend, Claire, to mind her own business," Frank said to MacKendrick.

"Give me a hand, guys," Billy Two Trees said to Frank and Joe as he tried to pull the pale, sweaty ranger to his feet. Frank and Joe helped him get MacKendrick to a standing position.

"I trusted you, Roger," the chief said sadly as he took MacKendrick to his truck.

"That was your first mistake," MacKendrick muttered.

Joe and Frank Hardy rode with Billy Two Trees to the hospital, where MacKendrick was admitted to the emergency room with a separated shoulder. They left the police chief and his ward in the lobby and headed for Owen Watson's room. They found a happy and healthy Owen there with his daughter and eagerly told them everything.

"So MacKendrick was secretly working for Carl Vissen." Owen Watson grinned as he sat up in his hospital bed and took the cup of ice water Wendy handed him.

"Yeah," Joe said. "Vissen must have been the one with the connections who got MacKendrick the job as ranger. So he had a debt to pay Vissen."

"It took a little hunting, but we found out about New Gehenna Partners," Frank told Owen. "Vissen wanted to strip mine the valley and clear all the timber."

"He and Mayor Latimer were funneling the state money into Vissen's operation," Owen said. "I had proof in my files. Now I know what they had in mind."

"Vissen and MacKendrick tried to make your shooting look like the Knights of Liberty did it,"

Joe said. "MacKendrick even injured himself and killed those sheep for the same reason."

Frank added, "MacKendrick knew what the Knights were doing, so he dressed up like one of them, when he did his dirty work, in case anybody saw him."

"But why didn't Vissen just go after what he wanted directly?" Wendy asked. "Why did he have to set us all against each other?"

"Smoke and mirrors," Frank said.

"The old magician's secret," Joe said. "Create a distraction so nobody sees how the trick works."

"If Vissen could set Owen and his group against the ranchers, the ranchers against the Knights of Liberty, and the Knights against Owen, the ranchers, and everybody else *but* Vissen, nobody would know what Vissen was doing until his deal was completely wrapped up," Frank concluded.

Joe added, "And if it was ever discovered, Vissen could pretend that he had nothing to do with it, because it looked as though he had been threatened. MacKendrick was behind that, too."

Wendy looked at Joe and Frank with barely disguised admiration. "If I didn't know better, I'd say you two have been mixed up in things like this before," she said.

"A little," Frank said.

Joe shrugged and added, "Once or twice."

* * *

The next day the local news crews crowded around the podium at the front of Gehenna Town Hall. Half a dozen microphones were taped to the lectern. Technicians switched on their lights, and video cameras whirred as Owen Watson stepped before the microphones.

Doreen Falk-Watson and Nick Krakowski stood on one side of Owen; Billy Two Trees stood on the other. Behind them, off to the side, stood Wendy with Joe and Frank.

"I'm sure by now you've all heard of the indictments being brought against Carl Vissen and Mayor Latimer for fraud and misappropriation of public funds," Owen began. "Chief Two Trees is continuing his investigation, and he will brief you after I'm done."

Owen continued. "What I'm here to tell you about is a new group that has been formed to lobby for the future of Gehenna Canyon. This fall a bill is being introduced in Congress to have this precious natural area designated as a national park. All of us in this town have been at war with each other over this issue. Now we realize that we cannot succeed unless we forget our petty differences and focus on what's important—protecting Big Bison River for our children and our children's children to use with respect."

There was a round of applause from the townspeople who had come to listen to the press conference.

Frank looked at Joe. Joe looked at Frank. Both

of them appeared uncomfortable. They knew where Owen's speech was headed. Neither brother liked to be in the public eye.

Frank and Joe turned to Wendy. She had the same expression on her face.

Owen continued his address. "Before I turn things over to Billy Two Trees and your questions, I'd personally like to thank my brave daughter, Wendy, and two remarkable young men who came in here as strangers, became the targets of a wave of terror, and managed to get to the bottom of the sordid mess that has caused so much pain and tension . . . Joe and Frank Hardy."

Owen looked around. His daughter and the Hardys had disappeared.

Within a half hour, Frank, Joe, and Wendy Watson were in a raft on Big Bison River, just about to go over the rapids at the center of Niagara Junior.

Frank and Joe's next case:

When Frank's old school friend Freddie Felix landed a job as a circus clown, he thought it was his big break. Now he's landed in big trouble instead. A suspicious fall has put him in the hospital, and the Hardys are determined to get to the bottom of it. They've decided to join the spectacle—a three-ring circus of crime! Under the big top, Frank and Joe uncover a mix of dirty deals and sinister secrets. And they face a deadly nemesis willing to use any weapon—from poisonous snakes to man-eating tigers—to put a quick end to their act. They may be dealing with a bunch of clowns, but this case is no joke because there's nothing funny about murder . . . in *High-Wire Act*, Case #123 in The Hardy Boys Casefiles™.